A MORETTI MEN HOLIDAY NOVELLA

MISTLETOE Masquerade

JILL RAMSOWER

Edits by: Editing4Indies
Photographer: Wander Aguiar
Model: Brady

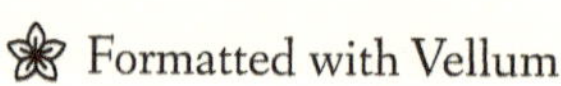 Formatted with Vellum

MISTLETOE MASQUERADE

JILL RAMSOWER

This one's for my momma—the Christmas baby who grew up to adore the season even though it meant her birthday was often overlooked. She shared with me a love for all things Christmas because she brought such joy to the holiday, and I hope this story brings a little festive fun to all of you.

"You want to hang out in a ballroom ... full of cops?" Sante Mancini stares at me like I've sprouted a second head. Of course, he would see it that way. He's in the Mafia, after all.

"Not just cops—*masked* cops ... in tuxedos!" I grin wickedly, enjoying his discomfort. Teasing him is so much more fun now that I know him better. In the past few months, I've become good friends with his wife, Amelie, who I met through my best friend Dani. The three of us girls are always together these days, which means I see their husbands quite a bit, as well.

Sante grimaces. "Doesn't sound like a Christmas party to me. More like a Halloween nightmare."

Before I can reply, Tommy jumps in. "But you were raised Buddhist, right? Buddhists don't celebrate Christmas." Tommy is Dani's husband. He often sees things in black and white, so explaining the intricacies of culture and religion isn't something I'm delving into right now.

"My parents are Buddhist. That doesn't mean I can't love all things Christmas," I offer vaguely, then turn back to Sante. "Which includes the annual policeman's ball when said ball is going to be a fancy holiday masquerade with glittery decorations in a gorgeous hotel ballroom."

"That ballroom can be fancy as fuck, but it's still gonna stink like a barn if it's full of pigs."

Amelie smacks his chest indignantly. "Hey! Not all cops are bad. Quit raining on her parade."

He gapes at his wife with a petulant innocence, as though he has no idea what he did to deserve her reprisal. The sight makes me chuckle.

"It's fine, Amelie. He can think whatever he wants. It doesn't change my opinion that it would be fun to finally attend one of these fancy parties instead of delivering food and leaving. The occupation of the other guests is irrelevant. And this event is a masquerade ball, so it would be even easier to pretend I'm just another guest."

"I think you should go for it," Dani chimes in. "It's not like they're going to arrest you for crashing the party."

"Agreed," Amelie says. "And like I said, they're not all bad. Malone is a good guy."

"Yes!" Dani's eyes widen. "And he is seriously pretty to look at. I can only imagine him in a tux."

Both men make faces as though they've just swallowed a spoonful of mud.

Sante raises his hand. "Hold up. Calling him a good guy is awfully generous. Let's just say he's not a total asshat."

I ignore Sante and grin at the girls. "A few months back, Sante took me home, and on the way, he stopped at the police station. He met up with a man in front of the building, and the guy was one yummy piece of man candy. I stayed in the car but could see the two of them. The guy had blond hair and a body that would make Superman weep. Is that him?"

"That's him," Amelie agrees. "A man-dy cane, if you will?"

All three of us girls burst into a fit of giggles while the guys roll their eyes.

"Seriously, Mel?" her husband groans.

She shrugs with a wry grin. "It's true. He's an absolute snack." She's getting a rise out of goading her husband, and he's too naturally possessive not to take the bait.

"I suppose if you like a Goody Two-Shoes who thinks his shit don't stink," Sante grumbles.

Tommy glares at his friend. "You're the one who practically has the guy on speed dial. Wouldn't be surprised if you sent him a Christmas card."

"Oh, now I gotta hear it from you, too. Is that it? Like you've never called the guy for a favor."

"A reciprocal swap of information isn't a favor," Tommy points out plainly.

"Poh-tay-to, poh-tah-to, Tommy. You needed intel, and he agreed to an exchange. Same difference."

I can tell Tommy wants to argue over the distinction in that technical way of his, but Amelie cuts him off.

"Sach, I think you should do it. And if you need a dress, I'll ask my sister if she's got anything you can borrow. They do samples for the holiday season ages in advance. I'm sure she's got something lying around."

Her sister is a badass fashion designer with her own label. As a sculptor, I'm an avid supporter of all the arts. Wearing one of Lina's dresses would be a dream come true.

"Oh my God. That would be incredible."

Amelie and Dani both clap their hands like giddy schoolgirls as a radiant grin splits my face.

At times like this, I wonder how I got so lucky to be a part of this makeshift family. It's a feeling I've never fully experienced. Not only are my parents on the opposite coast in California but having emigrated from Japan before I was born, they've always been difficult for me to relate to. Finding a sense of belonging here in New York has filled my heart with joy.

"I'm so doing this. Help me get an outfit, and I'll pretend I'm diplomatic royalty for a night, even if it means wearing a borrowed dress and changing in a grimy staff bathroom."

Amelie holds up her phone. "Commence Operation Mistletoe Masquerade." She dials her sister's number while I wiggle in my chair, and the guys both shake their heads before downing the rest of their drinks.

Those Scrooges can bah, humbug all they want.

This Santa's elf is going undercover for a night of festive mischief...

MY WATERMELONS ARE DISPLAYED on a table alongside artfully arranged assortments of peeled and cubed fruit. My sole responsibility is to carve the requested food items as specified and deliver them to the party. In this case, I carved poinsettias into the face of three large watermelons. I made sure they looked spectacular at one of the finger-food stations set up around the enormous ballroom, each supplied with row upon row of bubbling champagne flutes to ensure guests enjoyed themselves to the fullest.

The hotel has outfitted the room with glittering red-and-gold Christmas decor, along with a fully decked-out tree that stands at least fifteen feet tall. The white lights peeking from between ball ornaments and bows twinkle nearly as bright as the crystal sconces and chandeliers.

The room is a breathtaking holiday fantasy come to life.

I can't wait to get back in there now that I've changed out of my uniform and into my gown. I never dreamed I'd get the opportunity to wear something so luxurious when Amelie suggested calling her sister. I knew she designed clothing, but this gown belongs in another dimension.

Worthy of Mount Olympus, it's elegant and ethereal. Crafted of white chenille, the fabric is as smooth and flawless as freshly fallen snow. The one-shoulder design hugs my chest while draping gently down at my hips and acting as the perfect canvas for embroidered artistry unlike any I've ever seen—a cascade of vibrant red poinsettia flowers with forest green leaves from my shoulder, across my chest, and down the opposite side to the skirt hem. The appliqué blooms are accented with intricate stitching and a smattering of beads—enough to give the gown depth and sparkle, but not so much to weigh it down.

Add to it a white velvet mask with a matching poinsettia garnish, and I feel like a Christmas queen.

And that's precisely who I am tonight.

No one has to know the gown is borrowed, or that my invitation was technically a job order. And they won't, if I can just find a place to stash my boring black catering uniform. The dingy staff bathroom doesn't have a single nook or cranny I could use. I have to find a place on my way through the kitchen back to the ballroom.

You've got this, Sach.

I channel my inner diva and square my shoulders with the certainty that I am perfectly entitled to be here tonight and do exactly as I please.

One last glimpse of myself in the mirror is all I need.

Girl, you are fire!

I feel a solid inch taller, and when you're not even five foot, every inch makes a big difference. It could just be the insane stilettos I'm wearing.

Who's to say?

All that matters is I feel unstoppable. I'm ready to have a fabulous night.

I unlock the door and walk down a dark hallway, pausing only briefly to stash my bag in the employee locker room opposite the kitchen. Once that's done, I square my shoulders again and stroll confidently into the kitchen. Heads swivel in my direction until I feel an entire room full of eyes glued to me.

It's understandable. I'd stare at the woman wearing this dress, too, if I could. Hell, I did stare at my reflection when I first put on the mask. I didn't even recognize myself. The sophisticated woman staring back at me felt surreal. I was so amazed that I took a ridiculous number of selfies and maybe even spun in a circle. Twice.

Thankfully, no one stops me on my trip through the kitchen. And once I return to the ballroom, I see that the gathering has ballooned to a healthy throng of masked partygoers. The upper echelon of New York City law enforcement, along with their guests—all circulating animatedly without any idea that an impostor lurks among them.

Nothing all that bad would happen if they figured me out, but breaking the rules is exhilarating, nonetheless.

And for once, I get to be a part of the celebration.

As I take a glass of champagne from a refreshments table, I craft a story for myself. I'm a businesswoman—the owner of several prestigious art galleries. I arrived not by subway but in the back of a luxurious sedan owned by a car service I frequently employ. My dress is no longer a designer sample but a boutique purchase that is one of hundreds lining the closet in my extravagant Park Avenue apartment.

A titillating smile teases its way across my crimson-stained lips.

"I'd say 'a penny for your thoughts,' but with such a pretty smile, I'd be willing to pay a whole lot more." A middle-aged man who is way too tan for December grins at me slyly from behind a gawdy blue sequined mask as though he's all too aware of his wicked charm, having zero clue how close he's come to insinuating I'm a hooker.

I have to shake off my stunned disbelief, and as I do, all remnants of my kick-ass persona scatter right along with it.

What am I supposed to say to this guy? What if he's the chief of police or the police commissioner? Does he know I don't belong? Oh God. What am I doing here? Why on earth did I think this was a good idea?

Sachi, get a grip and answer the man!

"Um ... I was just appreciating the party. They did a great job."

Okay, not bad. Scrape yourself together. You got this.

"Yeah, they did good this year. The whole masquerade part is kinda fun, if you're into that sort of thing." His voice drops at the end with an icky insinuation like we're wearing blindfolds and ball gags instead of festive carnival masks.

What a weirdo.

"Themed parties can be great when everyone participates," I say merely to be polite.

His eyes spark hungrily. "Now you're talking. My favorite kind of party is the one where everyone gets involved. You like that sort of thing, too?"

Oh dear God.

Does this man think I'm talking about orgies? What the hell is wrong with him?

I'm about to make an excuse and disappear when another man approaches on my other side, effectively caging me in.

"Danny, tell me you're not torturing this beauty with your attempt at conversation." He leans in conspiratorially, whiskey wafting heavily on his breath and burning my eyes. "Thinks he's a player, but there's a reason guys like him are always single."

Then he winks, as though he's any better. The beefy man with white-blond highlights in his intentionally messy hair screams of insecurity.

"I take it you're not single, then?" I ask curiously.

"I am," he quickly reassures me. "But not like him, you know?"

Riiight.

"Yeah, Levitt, you just collect ex-wives like trading cards," the man named Danny jabs back.

"Sometimes things don't pan out." He shrugs, unbothered. "Means Mrs. Right is still out there somewhere, and when I find her, I'll treasure her forever." He holds my gaze with a hooded stare that I think he's hoping is seductive.

That, or he's trying to hold in a fart.

Could go either way.

This is not at all how I saw my evening going. I don't know what exactly I expected, but this wasn't it.

In fact, I'd say this is karmic retribution. The universe saw my antics and decided to put me in my place. I'm at a loss for how to describe the horrific misfortune of this situation.

"I should really..." I start to sidestep my way to an escape when an arm wraps around my waist and pulls me into a solid body.

"There you are. Thought I'd never find you in this crowd." The masked man lifts my hand to his lips and places a chaste kiss on the back of my fingers.

Eyes wide, heart thudding in my chest, I gasp in a breath that fills my lungs with the heady scent of spiced aftershave.

It only lasts a second.

An eternal heartbeat that lingers like smoke from an extinguished candlewick. I don't even have time to react. The touch is over before it began, and I have to quash an unnerving urge to grab his lapels and draw him in for a real kiss.

"Follow my lead," the man murmurs before pulling back and giving me a peek at the bluest eyes I've ever seen. He's the most devastatingly handsome man I've ever come across, and I can't even see his whole face behind the black domino mask. Broad, muscled shoulders are outfitted in a tuxedo jacket cut to his athletic form, crafted from black velour that exudes confident elegance. A chiseled jawline with a dusting of blond facial hair forms a five o'clock shadow. And those lips—a rosy color full of life and hitched in a wry smirk.

I'd probably follow this man off a cliff if he asked me to.

He is utterly captivating and undoubtedly familiar. I've seen him before. He's the man I saw with Sante. The detective the girls talked about days earlier. Malone—the man-dy cane.

Not only is he here but his large hand is curved around my waist, and his scent is melding its way into my DNA.

"Appreciate you guys entertaining my date, but I need to steal her away. Come on, kitten."

"Yes, Daddy." The words slip past my lips without an

ounce of forethought, and I'm reminded of the myriad of times my mother told me I was too sassy for my own good.

I can't believe I've just called this man Daddy in public, but what did he expect? He told me to follow his lead, right? And he called me kitten, after all.

Not only is he unfazed but I can tell Detective Malone doesn't ruffle easily by the seductive rumble of laughter that tickles my ear as we walk away from my now speechless companions.

"Careful, or you'll end up on the naughty list," he murmurs under his breath.

"I'm not the one running around kissing random women I've never met before."

"Touché. That part wasn't necessary, but I can't say I'm sorry."

"You might when you meet my husband."

He stops mid-step, eyes coming to mine, then flitting to my left hand. "You're married?"

It's my turn to smirk. "No, but you didn't know that."

A masculine sound of amusement resonates from his chest as his penetrating eyes bore into mine. "Let's clear all that up right now. Are you here with someone?"

"No," I say, transfixed by the ocean of aquamarine staring back at me.

"I suppose that still leaves the possibility that you have someone back home. Are you seeing anyone?"

"Why do you want to know?" My voice has gone breathy as my lungs forget how to function.

This gorgeous man leans in, his lips inches from my ear as he murmurs, "I've captured the attention of the most radiant woman in the room, and you want to know why I'd ask if she's single?"

"Well, when you put it like that..."

He pulls back enough for our eyes to lock, then raises a brow. He wants an answer.

"No, I don't have a date, nor am I seeing anyone."

His chin dips in a single nod before he takes my hand and leads us toward the drink table. He selects a glass of champagne and lifts it to clink with mine.

"To a night of unexpected delights."

2

Dean

Jesus, I sound as ridiculous as those assholes who had her cornered.

I don't typically pursue women at work events, but something about this woman has me feeling like I'll never forgive myself if I let her slip away.

The way my hand circles halfway around her tiny waist.

The aristocratic lift of her chin, and her elegant jawline that begs to be kissed.

The quick bite of her sassy words softened by the innate way she relaxes into my touch.

Regardless of the reason, this woman is worth a few broken rules.

We both drink to my toast, our eyes reluctant to break contact.

"What precinct are you with?" I ask, needing to know more about the woman who's captured my attention more so than anyone in a very long time.

"I'm not. I came with a friend, but we didn't make it inside before she started to get a migraine and decided to leave."

"And you stayed?" I'm surprised, considering she probably doesn't know anyone here.

Her answering smile is as serene as a sunrise walk on the beach. "I was already here with my mask in place. Seemed a shame to walk away."

Shame is right.

I'd been just as close to backing out of attending, but I've never been so goddamn glad to be in a tux as I am right now.

"And then you were accosted by those assholes." I know what I did was just as obnoxious, but I was nearby and heard everything they said. I couldn't stand by and leave her to that nightmare.

She gives a small laugh, and ripples of warmth radiate through my chest.

"I was definitely starting to question my decision to stay."

At that moment, a man walking through the crowd

jostles her from behind. Her free hand reaches for me, steadying herself by clinging to me, and fuck if my inner caveman doesn't beat his fists against his chest. I'm all for independent, confident women, so I have no clue why her relying on me for support feels so goddamn good, but it does.

"Excuse me," she says, lowering her gaze as though embarrassed.

I wrap my hand around her waist and draw her closer to my side to keep her out of harm's way. Social norms dictate that I should retract my hand now—I don't know this beautiful creature well enough to maintain such a possessive touch—but my arm refuses to cooperate. It's found a new home, curved protectively around her, and is threatening all-out mutiny at the prospect of being ousted.

She lifts her wide-eyed gaze to mine, her lips gently parting.

I briefly consider selling my soul for a taste of those lips. They're begging to be kissed, but I've taken enough liberties already. Instead, I drink in the sight of her and say, "I, for one, am grateful you decided to stay."

Her throat bobs with a swallow. "Me, too," she breathes.

I have no doubt she feels the intense chemistry between us just as acutely as I do.

The sparks of desire.

The combustible heat.

It electrifies the air around us.

I have to lift my gaze to break the contact because it feels like something might literally catch fire if I don't release this pressure.

"Quite the turnout," I offer. My ragged and frayed voice is shredded from restraint.

"The masquerade element draws people out."

"Any excuse to test the limits of good behavior." I should know, considering I walked up to a woman I've never met, kissed her hand, and called her kitten. I'm not sure what to think about that.

"Even with this crowd?" she asks, surprised.

"They say the psychology of a cop and a criminal often overlaps."

"Do you fall into that category?"

"Up until five minutes ago, I would have said no," I admit.

"But now?" she prods gently.

I've never taken a bribe or anything like it, but in recent months, I've found myself cooperating with men I should be arresting. It's a shift I didn't see coming. And with the indecent thoughts I'm fighting off regarding this woman in white, I'm wondering if I'm still the man I thought I was.

"I'm starting to realize that certain motivations might inspire even the best of men to act out of character. We're cops, not saints, after all." My voice takes on a husky tone when my gaze locks with hers.

Yet again, another partygoer clumsily invades our

personal space. I see it happening in slow motion and am able to spin us out of the way before either of us can be jostled. In the process, the raven-haired beauty ends up pressed flush against me.

A tiny gasp slips past her lips, drawing my eyes.

"Sorry about that. I didn't want her to spill your drink," I murmur distractedly. My thoughts are now fixated on her incredibly lush lips.

You're still clinging to her, asshole. Time to let go.

One frenetic heartbeat after another ticks by until I'm able to convince my hand to relax at her back, giving her the space to pull away. Except that doesn't happen. The dainty fingers of her free hand clutch my lapel while she holds her champagne out to the side. She doesn't budge an inch before peering up at me through a forest of thick black lashes and stunning me with three simple words.

"Dance with me."

3

Sachi

I wear Velcro kids' shoes with flashing lights and neon colors because I can—one of the perks of being short. I sculpt animals out of mashed potatoes when I eat at fancy restaurants and collect pictures I take of dogs I see at the park because I think they're cute.

I suppose it shouldn't come as a shock to me that I just asked a stranger to dance with me, yet I'm a bit flabbergasted at myself. Not a single person is dancing in the entire ballroom. I'm not even sure there's a dance floor. And I didn't just ask the man to dance, I practically demanded it.

The man I only know as Malone never even flinches.

He sets down our drinks on a nearby table, then guides me back into his arms. A small ensemble of musicians is playing an assortment of Christmas classics in a corner of the ballroom, filling the air with cheerful ambiance. The current number is a sultry rendition of "I'll Have a Blue Christmas Without You"—perfect for a romantic turn about the floor.

I adore the way I feel in Malone's confident hold. His one hand holds mine while his other hand rests at my lower back, keeping my body close to his.

I'm not sure which is more tantalizing.

The hand at my back radiates warmth to an already volcanic heat building in my center, while the skin-on-skin contact of our joined hands sends bolts of liquid lightning through my veins enough to power the entire Christmas tree in Rockefeller Center.

"Considering I'm pretending to be your date," Malone begins as we gently sway in tandem, "surely, it's not too forward to ask your name."

Name? Oh my God.

I've been so caught up that I completely forgot he doesn't have any clue who I am. Not that I know him all that well, but I knew *of* him, and I had a name. I could be Joan of Arc for all he knows, and he certainly has no idea I'm friends with Sante and Tommy.

A sliver of unease trickles down my spine.

It's fine, Sach. None of that matters. This is just a dance —a single night of fun, okay?

Absolutely. Right. No reason to worry.

"Sachi," I offer, keeping my last name to myself. "And you are?" I ask because he doesn't need to know that I know, but I also have no clue whether Malone is a first or last name. Hell, my memory could suck, and I could have the wrong guy altogether.

"Dean Malone. It's an absolute pleasure to meet you, Sachi. Of course, I hope you're aware that half this room probably knows you called me Daddy by now."

I was right. He is Malone, and that's his last name. Good to know.

"A tough guy like you can handle a little ribbing, right?" I fight back a grin.

"I tell you what," he says, then pulls me closer—close enough that our bodies graze one another. "You call me whatever you want, so long as you're calling me."

Oh *damn.*

He's good. Like, really freaking good.

Because despite the corniness of his lines, the sincerity in his voice has me gobbling up every word.

Tonight was supposed to be a simple indulgence—a little fun and a good story—but I get the feeling something big is being set into motion, and I don't want it to stop. I'm enjoying myself with a man more than I have in ... maybe ever.

The realization and his candid appreciation of me gives me a wealth of confidence. I feel desirable and bold and effervescent. Eyes follow us as we sway together from one song into the next, talking quietly about everything and nothing. We're discussing the optimal height of the perfect snowman when a voice lances through our conversation.

"Malone! I thought you said you came alone." A young guy in his early twenties stops beside us, interrupting our moment with an impressive degree of cluelessness. If "wet behind the ears" was literal, he'd have puddles at his feet from being so earnestly naive.

"Eckerman." Dean nods curtly, keeping his hand at my lower back. It's a tad possessive, considering we hardly know one another, but I'm not mad about it. His comforting strength feels too good to resent. "This is Sachi. Sachi, our newest officer, Ralph Eckerman."

The unmasked man grins proudly and extends his hand. "Pleasure to meet you." His grip is firm, though the shake lasts a smidge longer than is customary. It's purely unintentional. He's just so dang enthusiastic that I have to laugh.

"Good to meet you, too."

"Speaking of dates, Eck, where's your wife?" Dean asks abruptly. He doesn't seem nearly as entertained by the momentary interruption.

Ralph motions over his shoulder. "Bathroom."

Dean lifts his chin. "You should probably get back to her. Wouldn't want to get separated in this crowd."

"Oh yeah. Right." The recruit winks with a grin. "You two enjoy your evening." He disappears with a wave.

"He's kind of adorable in a golden retriever sort of way," I muse aloud.

Dean narrows his eyes and pulls me back into our dance hold. "I suppose, if you like that sort of thing." His huffy response is endearing because it bears a hint of humor that softens the jealousy.

"You work together?"

"Not exactly. I'm a detective, and he's a beat cop, but he's sort of latched onto me." His wry tone has a humorous undercurrent, like he wants to be grumpy, but he's just too decent to let it fully take hold.

I bite back a smile. "I thought this event was for higher-ups."

"His father's a captain at another precinct."

"Ah."

He makes a rumbling noise in agreement that causes a flutter deep in my chest.

"He gets preferential treatment," I observe, curious about Dean's thoughts on the matter.

"Maybe some, but he's actually a decent cop, just green."

"And you? What kind of detective are you?"

The musicians launch into a lively instrumental of "Rocking Around the Christmas Tree," though the upbeat music barely registers in my ears. I'm too intent on hearing Dean's reply. He's intriguing in a way I can't define but has me hanging on every word he says.

"I'm the persistent kind of detective."

I appreciate his choice of descriptors. He didn't say something generic like "I'm a good detective" or "veteran detective" or list the awards he's received. He chose to share what he sees as admirable, and to him, that's persistence—something I imagine is rather crucial in solving crime.

He's persistent and perceptive and generous and deliciously self-assured—all qualities that would serve him well as a detective. They also have the potential to make him an incredible lover. What I wouldn't give to test that theory...

Holy hell, am I really considering that?

Am I willing to have sex with a man I hardly know?

I've never had a one-night stand. It always seemed a little risky to be so vulnerable with a man I don't know. Being quirky and impulsive about my wardrobe or hobbies is one thing. Having sex with a stranger is a whole other level of courage.

But this guy's a cop—one my friends seem to think is a decent guy.

Maybe this is my chance to have my cake and eat it, too.

Man-dy cane cake.

Mmm...

I lick my suddenly parched lips.

Dean leans in close to my ear. "You do realize you just broadcasted every last thought that passed behind your expressive eyes. You're definitely going on Santa's naughty list."

"Do you think he'll cuff me for being bad?" If it wouldn't make me look a smidge crazy, I'd take a look around to see where that saucy statement came from because I know it can't be me.

And the hunger in my raspy voice? Where did this sexy vixen come from, and can I keep her?

Dean's hand releases mine before cupping the back of my neck, his entire body going stiff. "Careful, kitten. You're adding to an already ... *sensitive* situation."

The realization that I'm arousing this gorgeous man beyond the point of his control intoxicates me. I want more. I *need* more. So much so that I don't have the capacity to overthink my actions. The only thing on my mind is getting more of Dean.

I allow my body to drift lazily across his, reveling in the feel of his hardening length as it grazes my lower belly.

"Then maybe we should leave," I suggest in a breathy whisper.

Holy shit, I can't believe it.

I did it.

I just offered myself up for a night of what promises to be off-the-charts sex with a man I hardly know. Never have I ever been so forward or brazen. Nor have I ever been so grateful. I want this man.

I want to be his for the night. I want it so badly that I'm a tangled knot of every emotion possible as I wait for his response.

Just one perfect night.

That's all I'm asking...

4

Dean

*T*HEN *MAYBE WE SHOULD LEAVE.*

I can hardly believe my own ears.

This breathtaking, captivating woman wants me to take her home and do wicked things to her. She's offered herself to me, and I'm more than ready to take whatever she's willing to give.

My hand tightens reflexively around the back of her neck.

"Your place or mine?" As if I would pass up this opportunity.

Forget the party.

I made my appearance, so my boss can hardly complain. The rest of the night is mine to enjoy. And goddamn, am I going to devour every minute.

"Yours." Her answer bears a slight tremble, and I wonder if it's nerves or excitement. Probably both.

While I'm not nervous, the fire in my blood definitely has me on edge.

I take her hand and spin us toward the exit.

I can't believe my luck that this divine creature was here alone and stumbled right into my path. Like we were meant to find one another. It's ridiculous. I don't believe in fate, but the course of events tonight makes a man wonder.

The second we're beyond the ballroom, I whirl around and seize her lips with mine. It's what I've desperately wanted to do since first laying eyes on her. I couldn't wait another minute, and the taste of her is just as heady as I suspected. Champagne laced with strawberries and mint —sweet with a tangy edge—the same as her.

She meets each stroke of my tongue with one of her own.

Bold yet graceful—she's absolutely breathtaking.

I pull away only because the masks are getting in our way. That, and I want to see her. All of her.

Careful not to mar her hair, I remove her mask, then mine, and we take each other in for the first time. I didn't think the mask had hidden much, but I was wrong. She's even more spellbinding now that I see the elegant angle of her high cheekbones. I'd say Sachi should be on billboards if it wouldn't mean every man in the world pining for her.

"You are the most stunning woman I've ever seen." It's the truth, and I have to tell her. I want her to know exactly how I feel.

"Kiss me, Dean." Her breathy words clench tight around my balls and have me surging forward to do her bidding. I love that she's not afraid to ask for what she wants. And what I want is to devour every inch of her. I want to sink myself inside her and feel her writhe beneath me until she's screaming my name.

Jesus, I need to get us out of here before I end up fucking her in a hotel bathroom.

I pull back again, this time admiring her kiss-swollen lips and the point at the base of her neck where her skittering pulse flutters with excitement. She's the most alluring, sensual woman I've ever known, and I need more. *Now.*

"Let's get your coat." I take her hand and turn, leading her toward the coat check station.

"I don't have one with me. My friend ended up taking it home with her."

I pause and peer back at her, confusion wrinkling my brows. "It's fifteen degrees outside."

Her cheeks flush. "I know ... it was silly of me..."

I lift her chin with a gentle touch of my knuckles to bring her gaze back to mine. "It's fine." I shrug out of my tux jacket and hold it out for her. "I'm plenty warm without this."

"Thank you."

She smiles up at me with such genuine gratitude that I want to march her back inside the ballroom and demand that whatever magistrate is present marry us on the spot. It's the most ludicrous, absurdly impulsive notion I've ever had, and I'm stunned at how reasonable it sounds in my head.

What the fuck has come over me?

It's lust. I must have gone too damn long without getting laid.

Or not. Maybe Sachi's simply that incredible.

Either way, I need to get her home and fuck her senseless so that my oxygen-deprived brain can get some blood flowing to it again. The little bit of focus I have left right now is centered on making sure my dick doesn't tent my pants.

Once we reach the valet, I hold her body against mine, her back to my front, to ensure the frigid air doesn't chill her. And to hide the fact that I'm losing the battle with my dick. Even the crystalized flurries in the frozen air aren't enough to shrink his excitement. The sweet scent of berries and cream coming from Sachi's hair isn't helping.

When my black unmarked Dodge Charger pulls around, I breathe a sigh of relief. I help her into the passenger seat, then hurry back to the driver's side.

"The heat okay?" I adjust the settings, which the valet

has set to maximum, then pull out of the drive-through and into city traffic.

"Yeah, I'm good."

"If that changes, let me know."

"Yes, sir."

The words linger in the thickening air.

My eyes cut hungrily to her. She stares back, eyes rounding before she bites her bottom lip to fight back a grin.

Fuck, she's adorable, and she's not even trying.

A smirk hooks the corner of my lips as I shake my head and turn my attention back to the road. "I'd love for you to tell me more about yourself."

"Like what?"

"Like what you do for a living and how long you've been in the city. You don't have a local accent, so I assume you aren't from here."

"I'm originally from California. My parents are still there."

"That's quite the shift. What made you decide to leave the West Coast?"

"Art. I'm a ... I mean, I own a gallery."

"Really? That's impressive. Is it a family business?" She's young to own a gallery all by herself, but stranger things have happened.

"No, not family, but it's not just mine. It's ... complicated." She looks down at her hands—a sign I take to mean she's not crazy about the subject matter, so I detour the conversation.

"Rumor has it there may be a Nor'easter snowstorm coming for Christmas."

"Really?" She perks up, excitement brightening her eyes. "A white Christmas would be amazing."

"I agree now that my job doesn't require me to be out in the elements."

"Oh, yeah. I didn't think about that. Did you get stuck working out in storms very often?"

"Not often, but more than I would've liked," I answer in a playful tone. "It doesn't matter how many layers you wear when it's negative ten outside. Early on, I was too dumb to use those heat packs and thought I was going to lose my toes after directing traffic in a storm. The worst part was warming back up."

"You have to do it slowly, or it'll hurt." Her words hang in the air. While I don't think she initially meant to make a play on words, the double entendre can't be ignored.

We glance at one another, and her eyes widen with surprise.

Amusement hooks my lips into a crooked smile. "Definitely don't want it to hurt."

She coughs to hide a chuckle. "Not when it doesn't have to, though a tiny bit of burn never hurt anyone." Her eyes cut to mine again, and the desire in her stare has me forgetting to breathe.

Fuck.

Me.

Christmas has come early. I have no idea what I've done to deserve this woman, nor do I care. I don't want to question any of it and risk breaking the spell.

I hit the accelerator, drawing a giggle from beside me. It only takes another minute before we arrive at my building. Neither of us says much while we park and ride the elevator up to my apartment. There's no room for words with the sexual tension billowing all around us. Every second that ticks by ratchets up the pressure. My heart thuds a primal beat against my inner ear, and my lungs burn with the need for oxygen. The need for Sachi.

When I finally open my apartment, I watch her with curiosity as she takes in the sight.

My place is big. And nice. *Very* nice.

I prefer not to take dates home with me because it inevitably raises questions, but I could hardly back out when she took me up on the offer to come here. I want this too damn much to worry about what she might think about my money.

As I watch her taking in her surroundings, I'm struck by how much I enjoy seeing her here in my space. How much I want her to stay. I could see myself curled up with her on a rainy day, watching movies from the sofa. It's madness. I don't know her well enough to want things like that, yet the thoughts surface unbidden. I can't deny the urge is there.

As are other more ... pressing ... urges.

I close the distance between us, stopping inches behind her, and slip my jacket off her shoulders. She shivers.

"Cold?" I ask in a gruff, lust-filled murmur.

"Not even a little." Her face turns back toward mine, heat blazing in her eyes.

For the first time in my life, I feel a twinge of understanding for the monsters I hunt down and arrest because I sense I might be capable of depraved, unholy things if it would mean seeing that look in her eyes again and again.

"I need to fuck you, Sachi." I know I shouldn't be so blunt, but I can't help myself.

I *need* her.

"I think I'd like that very much." Her voice is a sensual caress against my skin.

She reaches behind her to unzip her dress. With her back still facing me, I see her fingers tremble too badly to cooperate. I take her hands in mine and lower them to her sides.

"You sure this is what you want?"

Please, Christ, say yes.

Something about this seductive, confident woman being so profoundly affected by me makes me want her even more. I want to explore every little reaction she has to my touch, but I want it to be voluntary. That's nonnegotiable.

"I do ... it's just, I don't normally do this sort of thing." She wrings her hands together. "I know it may have sounded like I do, but I don't, and you're so confident and ... and beautiful and ..."

I coax her to face me. "You don't normally have sex or go home with men you've just met?" I need to understand what's happening here. I don't want to fuck this up.

"The second one."

I nod. "Well, let me put your worries to rest. I'm going to make you feel very, very good, Sachi. Do you want to take things slowly?"

She nibbles on her bottom lip, then shakes her head. "I really want you to fuck me."

Thank *Christ*.

I place my hands on either side of her head, noting the faintest tremble of my own hands. "I don't want to be gentle," I admit in a heavy rasp.

Sachi's eyes hold mine steadfastly.

"Then don't."

5

Sachi

DEAN SEALS OUR DEAL WITH A KISS SO PASSIONATE
that his demanding need obliterates my remaining fears.
I'm swept away by a wave of consuming hunger. I want to
cry out with relief when his hands ease down the zipper
on my dress because, as much as I love the gown, I'm
desperate to get it off.

Desperate for his clothes to be off.

For the feel of our bodies pressed together with
nothing between us.

I fumble with the buttons on his dress shirt, our

tongues still dueling in a battle of desire before he pulls away and wrenches the shirt apart.

Buttons clatter to the wood floor.

Our connection broken, I take a moment to admire the taut curves of his muscled chest and the smattering of blond hair that makes him so damn masculine. So irresistible.

"If that dress isn't on the floor in three seconds flat, I'm ripping the damn thing off you." The dim lamp light glints off his steely eyes like shards of molten glass.

His unabashed hunger for me infuses my bloodstream with confidence.

I ease the single strap off my shoulder, unhurried by his threat. I want to tease out every ounce of his need— stoke that fire and see how high it will burn.

I'm not disappointed.

When the ivory fabric finally pools at my feet, I swear I can feel the heat from his stare sear my skin.

"Like what you see?" I ask brazenly. I wasn't wearing a bra, so I'm standing before him in nothing but a nude thong and red heels.

Dean's gaze doesn't detour from its ravenous perusal of my body. "No, I don't." His eyes finally lift to mine as he slips his shirt off. "Boys *like* what they see. I'm wondering how I could ever appreciate another sunset after seeing such beauty."

My lungs.

They've forgotten how to breathe.

No one has ever said anything so moving to me in my life. And with such earnest honesty. He's truly captivated by everything about me, and it makes me feel like I can fly. I want to capture the feeling and harness it to keep it with me always.

His hands reach for my hips, then slowly drift down as he lowers himself to squat and unbuckle the delicate ankle straps on my red heels. He shows surprising dexterity with such large hands. Tenderness despite his strength.

How very promising for things to come.

When he returns to his feet, he slides off his belt with a single commanding tug and lets it fall to the floor. He then lifts me into his arms, his hands on my backside, coaxing my legs around his hips. I take the opportunity to find his lips again, kissing him deeply as he takes us out of the entry and to the living room.

He supports my weight effortlessly—one of the advantages of our size difference. Now that my heels are off, he's a full foot taller than me and easily double my weight. That sort of disparity has made me uneasy around some men in the past, but not with Dean. He wields himself in a way that makes his size feel safe rather than threatening.

That sense of security is empowering.

Intoxicating.

I flex my hips to press myself against his hard length, still tucked away in his pants but straining up to reach me. Talk about a tease. He's so thick and solid ... and just out of my reach.

Frustration leaves me by way of a moan.

Dean nips at my bottom lip. "What is it, kitten? You need to feel my cock?" He sets me down, my ass balanced on the back of the sofa. "Is this what you want?" He works his hips to rub himself up and down against my center.

The sensation sends a blossoming warmth through my body that has me clambering for more. It's an offering of crumbs when I see the whole feast just out of reach.

"Feels so good, but I need more, Dean."

He makes a disapproving tsking sound. "So impatient." He reaches between us and unbuttons his pants, letting them fall to his feet, then leans in to suck my breast into his mouth, nipping at the tip with exquisite tension that has my head rolling back.

My clit swells and pulses.

When he switches to my other breast, he grinds against me again, this time with nothing between us but the thin fabric of our underwear.

"Oh God. *Yes.*"

The enhanced feel of him has me hurdling toward a release I can hardly comprehend.

It's too soon.

This never happens. But my muscles all clench, and my breaths hitch in my throat.

"You're going to come for me already, aren't you? Such a good girl." He nips at my breast again, intensifying the graze of his teeth over my nipple, and it's exactly what I need to seize hold of orgasmic bliss.

My thighs squeeze tight around his hips as I release a cry of ecstasy.

"Oh, baby girl. You're in trouble."

Dean's gravelly words tease at my consciousness, still muddled as I drift on the waves of release.

"Huh?"

"Making you come might be my new favorite hobby." He eases my feet to the floor and turns me to face the back of the couch, gently holding me steady in my disoriented state.

Once I'm securely holding the sofa, he kicks off his shoes and disappears from behind me for a moment. I hear a tear of foil, and a renewed tingle of excitement trickles down my spine.

I need this man inside me. *Now*.

Orgasms are fabulous, but there's nothing like the feel of being well fucked.

When I sense him return to me, I arch my back to press my entrance toward him in invitation.

"*Fuck*, kitten. You couldn't be any more perfect."

He accents his words with an appreciative squeeze of my ass cheek. I've always been a bit wistful that I didn't have more junk in the trunk, but the way he hisses at the contact tells me he's not bothered one bit.

His wide palm gives my ass a sudden smack that has me gasping and arching in pleasure.

I'm thinking about how my panties must be absolutely drenched when he promptly rips off the offending fabric.

His body bends forward to align with mine—his front to my back—and the scalding heat of his cock teases my entrance.

"Lift onto your toes," he rasps.

I do as I'm told, and he guides himself inside me a couple of inches.

A tremble wracks his body.

"Don't want to ... rip you apart ... but ... *fuck*, you feel so damn good." His ragged words stroke my skin with their praise and help me relax against the intense fullness filling me.

"Keep going." My encouragement is shaky and breathless, but he listens, nonetheless.

Soon, Dean is fully sheathed inside me.

The arm circling my middle leaves me as he rises upright and takes hold of my hips, his strong hands grasping me just shy of bruising.

"Hold tight, beautiful."

The growled words are the only warning I have before he pulls back, then impales me with a single thrust, followed by another, and another, until he's fucking me with a savage intensity.

Sometimes during sex, I have to focus on the sensations to stoke them forward, but with Dean, I couldn't control the wildfire raging inside me if I had to. He's in command, and my body has sworn fealty to obey only him. I am simply along for the ride.

And what a magnificent ride it is.

Already sensitive from my orgasm, the bundle of nerves inside me shimmers and sparks with an impending eruption of pleasure. The slap of Dean's body against mine mimics my pounding heartbeat. And every delicious thrust is accented by his balls colliding with my clit.

I'm seconds from succumbing to what might be the most mind-altering orgasm I've ever experienced when everything stops, and I'm suddenly empty.

"Wha—?" My incoherent moan earns me a wicked chuckle.

"I'm not nearly ready for this to be over. Come with me." Dean takes my hand and guides me around the sofa, positioning me on my back, then walking away.

Wondering what he's up to sends a giddy lightness through my chest.

My heart stumbles drunkenly around in my rib cage, nearly falling flat on its face when I hear the clink of a belt buckle being lifted off the wood floors.

The tiniest sliver of fear spikes my bloodstream, adding to the intoxicating cocktail of emotions, but I forget everything when Dean returns, and I'm treated to the unabashed sight of his naked body for the first time.

The man.

Is.

Spectacular.

There truly are no words for his brand of perfection. Dean is the physical embodiment of masculinity. Of predatory grace. Each sculpted muscle flexes with restrained power as he moves, his actions dripping with a natural dominance.

I watch raptly as his adept hands somehow form a double loop with the belt.

"Hands above your head." He rests a knee on the sofa cushion next to me while securing the belt around my proffered wrists. Once he's happy with the restraint, he guides my bound hands to rest on the cushions above my head. "Keep those exactly where they are, understood?"

"Yes, sir," I breathe.

An animalistic growl tears from his throat as he slams his lips against mine, possessing my mouth with a need so primal, it speaks to me on a cellular level.

My knees fall open, begging for his attention.

Dean's kiss travels down to my chest as he repositions himself over me. My body writhes with his touch. And when his tongue finally takes a languorous lick along my slit, I have an almost out-of-body experience.

"Yesss, Dean. God, it feels so good."

He groans against my flesh. I adore the sounds he makes—like he's not just getting off on eating me out but has found his own personal heaven between my thighs.

For the briefest second, I panic over the impending loss of this moment.

How can this possibly be a one-time thing?

I've never experienced sex like this. Never so overwhelmingly intense. Will I ever find this again, or is this the only time I'll ever know such all-consuming lust?

The thoughts are thunderous clouds lurking all around, but Dean's touch is the sun that fights off the rain. Before long, I'm lost in the bliss of that orgasm he's been teasing me with.

"So close..." I moan.

My legs twitch.

Tingles erupt in my center.

Dean pulls away.

"*No*! I just need a little more, *please!*"

"You'll come when I'm ready for you to come." He nips at my inner thigh before rising and removing the belt from my hands. In one swift motion, he lifts me and repositions us so that he's sitting low on the sofa, and I'm straddling his hips.

Up above him, I feel powerful. Divine.

I feel like I rule the world, and the glint in his eyes tells me that at this moment, I do rule his world.

I reach up and remove the rubber band and clips holding my hair in place. Long black swaths of hair cascade down all around me.

"If you were any more beautiful, it would be illegal," he says on a reverent breath.

"Would you lock me up, then?"

"Might lock you up anyway." His hands squeeze my hips. "Now, ride my cock and squeeze me until I can't see straight."

He helps guide his shaft deep inside me as I impale myself on him.

I feel so damn full in this position. It's almost too much.

Almost.

But not quite.

The pressure skates on the edge of pleasure and pain, leaning into the pleasure with every rock of my hips. He groans as I gain momentum, taking what I want from him. But I quickly realize I'm no more in control than I was before when he clasps my hips and begins to fuck me from below, using my body for his pleasure, and mine.

The gleam in his eyes is positively feral. It's the hottest thing I've ever seen.

"You take me so good, kitten." His words are spoken between panted breaths.

I have to brace my hands on his shoulders to steady myself. My modest breasts bob and bounce with the pounding thrusts. The sight of them, along with his chiseled abs clenching tight below, is such a turn-on that I'm now rocking with his motions and matching his intensity.

"Pinch those perfect pink nipples for me, Sachi. Show me how good it feels."

I keep one hand anchored against him and use the other to tease myself. My lips part wider as I gasp from the cataclysmic storm building inside me.

It's too much.

Inconsolable.

Uncontrollable.

I feel my very existence unraveling as the pounding in my ears heralds the approach of something apocalyptic.

Taking one last look at Dean, I try to sear the vision of him, muscles flexed—restraint warring with desire—into my brain so that I can take some tiny piece of this night with me.

"Oh God. *Dean!*"

"Yes, baby. Say my name when you come on my cock."

"*Say it*," he roars.

"Dean."

"Say it louder. I want the whole goddamn city to hear who you belong to."

"*Dean!*" I cry at the top of my lungs, propelled into an orgasm so intense that my vision darkens and my ears can no longer hear through the ringing.

"Fuck, *yes*." Dean joins me, pumping into me with two claiming thrusts.

I lean forward, too limp to stay upright, and rest my head in the crook of his neck. When my hearing returns, I'm treated to the sated sound of our panting breaths filling the empty night air.

"So fucking perfect."

I wonder if the intensity of our connection has enabled him to read my mind because his awe-filled murmur is precisely what I'm thinking.

So fucking perfect.

And I know deep in my bones no other man will ever measure up.

6

Dean

I carry Sachi to my bedroom with her legs wrapped loosely around my middle and her head resting in the crook of my neck. I'm not ready for our night to end. Hell, I didn't even want to take my dick out of her.

I thought fucking her would douse the flames of my desire, but it only whetted my appetite for more. I don't know how she feels about it, but the chemistry we have is unlike anything I've experienced before. From the moment our eyes first met back in the ballroom, I felt the pull of an invisible string tethering us together. I've told myself over and over that once I have a little more of her, this intense craving will subside.

Once we talk...

Once we kiss...

Once we fuck...

I've now buried myself so deep inside her I probably rearranged a few internal organs, and—spoiler alert—the craving is stronger than ever.

So when I tell myself that a couple more rounds tonight is all I need before I send her on her way, I know for a fact it's complete bullshit. Why would I ever voluntarily let go of something so extraordinary as the connection we share?

Why do I have to let her go?

Because she may not want more. But what if she does?

Surely, I can convince her to give me her number. One night isn't enough for me.

I hope to hell she feels the same.

I set her down in the primary bathroom and gently sweep the hair out of her face.

"Go to the bathroom while I clean myself up, then you're getting in bed with me." I don't ask because I don't want her to tell me no.

"You want me to stay?" Her groggy question is so damn adorable.

"Yeah, we'll get some sleep, and I can take you home in the morning." I kiss her temple, and she smiles up at me before closing herself in the small room that houses the toilet.

Once we're both ready, I guide her to the bed and pull back the covers. She gets in, scooting to the middle to give me room. I get in beside her, pulling her into the curve of my body.

She's so fucking tiny.

I hate to think of her being out in the city on her own without someone to protect her. I know it's misogynistic. She's not weak or helpless just because she's small, but my protective instinct doesn't care about modern logic. My job has given me too many opportunities to see what the monsters who call themselves men can do to women.

Locking her up sounds better and better.

You could always lock her down, instead.

Make her mine?

Mmm...

An overwhelming sense of satisfaction blankets me, despite the absurdity of such a thought after one goddamn night.

Regardless, she and I will talk in the morning. I'll fuck her first, just to make sure she's nice and agreeable, then I'll get her number. From there, it's anyone's guess.

I nuzzle my nose into her silky hair and inhale its sweet scent. "Get some sleep, kitten."

"*Mmm* ... yes, Daddy." Her playful purr wounds its way around my heart and squeezes.

Lock her down. Lock her up. I don't care what works so long as I get more of her. Now.

"Oh, Sachi. You can't go saying things like that and expect me to leave you alone." I slide my hand down between her legs and relish the way her back arches at my touch.

"So tired," she murmurs, though there's a smile dancing on her words.

I give her clit a sensual little pinch. Sachi gasps. I slide a finger deep inside her.

"Sleep will have to wait."

When Dean informed me that I was staying the night, I was still too sex-drunk to argue. I'm lying here with his warm body wrapped around mine, and reality is setting in.

I just had mind-bending sex with Detective Malone. Twice.

But it was more than that. We have a true connection unlike anything I've experienced before. The first-time awkwardness never happened. It was like we'd known each other for ages. He was charming and funny and made me feel like I hung the moon.

He even has Christmas decorations!

Seriously. What single man puts up a Christmas tree? None.

A pit forms in my stomach as an insidious tendril of doubt takes root in my mind.

What if he isn't single? What if I'm the other woman?

Maybe that's how a detective can afford such a gorgeous apartment. I really hate how much sense that makes. But surely the ladies would have mentioned if he was taken.

Not if they assumed you'd never betray them by sleeping with a cop.

Would they see it like that? I'm not sure. And what about Dean? He has no idea who my friends are. Would it bother him to know? Would he still be interested in me if he did?

Whoever said he was interested in anything more than a night?

Maybe that's all this should be. A single spectacular memory of a night I'll never forget.

A poisonous ache spreads from my chest and into my limbs, filling my veins with liquid lead. I weigh just as much as I did five minutes ago, but I feel heavier. Immovable.

I don't want to go.

I've never felt a connection like this with a man. It wasn't supposed to go like this tonight, but now that it has, how can I walk away?

How can you be okay putting your friends at risk by dating a cop?

My friends are my family.

What if something I say or do puts them in jeopardy of being thrown in jail?

I imagine telling my friends about Dean. Would the guys make their wives distance themselves from me if I was in a full-scale relationship with a cop? Probably. How could they not, considering who they are? And if that's the case, am I willing to lose them?

My heart constricts painfully.

Dani is my very best friend in the world. No sex is worth losing her over.

This was supposed to be a bit of fun. One night of pretend. That's all he was probably interested in anyway. I need to accept that it's best for everyone if I leave.

A single tear trails from my eye onto Dean's pillow.

I lie awake for two whole hours before I slip out of bed and collect my things. I wait to zip my dress and don't bother putting on my shoes.

Dean doesn't wake.

The security system isn't armed.

The universe is telling me to make my escape, so that's what I do. I should be relieved, yet I feel more desolate with every step I take.

I suppose it's only fitting that the best night of my life is also the worst—two sides of the same coin. And I'll take it because a night with Dean was worth the pain of losing him.

8

Dean

SHE'S GONE.

Motherfucker.

When I woke alone, I went straight to the living room to search for Sachi, but she's not here. And all her things are gone. It's like the entire night was a figment of my imagination.

I don't even know her last name.

The only evidence I have of our night together is what looks like mascara-stained tears dried into my pillow. Why would Sachi have been crying? Why did she sneak out in the night?

I never implied I wanted her gone because I didn't ... want her ... to go.

And I know she enjoyed herself just as much as I did. A woman can't fake the way she creamed all over my dick. So why disappear without a note or anything?

She told me she wasn't in a relationship. Would she have lied about that? I don't want to think she would, but I don't truly know her well enough to say for certain.

My frustration and disappointment sour with anger. I don't want to think poorly of Sachi or mar the memory of our night, but why else would she disappear?

Let it go, dickhead. She obviously doesn't want more.

I don't like it, but there's nothing more I can do, so I head to the shower. All I can think about as I scrub down is that I should be washing her ... and taking her against the shower wall. We were supposed to have the morning together.

No. I will *not* let it go.

If I were in the habit of letting things go, I wouldn't be the detective that I am. I've never once stopped chasing something just because it was out of reach, so I'm not about to start now. I know I can locate her. I may not like what I find when I do, but I can cross that bridge when I come to it.

The department had a guest list for security purposes. Her first name isn't common, so surely, I can at least get her last name and go from there.

I finish getting cleaned up with renewed purpose and

head to work. It's Sunday, but the station will still be full of folks on duty. I spend half an hour making calls until I track down someone with access to the gala guest list. Once it's emailed to me, I scour the names.

No Sachi.

Nothing even close to that name appears on the list.

I'm a little stunned. Did she lie about her name? She could have been a last-minute change, but it still seems odd. Even more importantly, finding her just got a lot damn harder. I'd be lying if I claimed the challenge didn't intensify my desire to track her down. When an investigation leads to more questions than answers, that's a sign to keep digging. Should I follow that philosophy when it comes to Sachi? Or am I just a desperate asshole clinging to something that wasn't meant to be?

I'm slouched in my office chair, trying to swallow a harsh dose of reality when a fellow detective strolls in.

"Malone, you're not going to believe this."

"I'm all ears." Whatever he has to say has got to be better than listening to my own depressing thoughts. Plus, Briggs is working with me on an investigation into a gang leader known as The Reaper. We've been trying to get intel on this guy for months. News on the case would be a welcome distraction.

"We got a successful trace on Reaper. We'll need to check things out first, but I have an address."

"Fuck yes. Show me what you've got."

9

Sachi

I have zero energy, and it has nothing to do with how much sleep I got, which wasn't much. Even a shower this morning did nothing to perk me up. It took everything I had to run by the hotel and retrieve the bag I'd stashed away last night. I should be blissfully ecstatic about my multiple orgasms. I should be on the phone texting my friends all the details of my wild night, but instead, I'm hiding at home with my curtains drawn.

I'm not ready to share my night for multiple reasons.

First, I don't want to tell my friends I slept with Dean —the man they know as Detective Malone. If I tell them about the sex but lie and say I never got the man's name, they'll demand to know why. It's simply easier not to tell them about it at all.

Second, reliving the events only makes my heart hurt worse than it does already. The sooner I move on, the faster I'll recover. Wallowing in the past, no matter how spectacular it was, will only bring me sorrow. To revel in the memory of the way I felt with Dean...

The spark.

The intensity.

The way he commanded my body like he knew exactly how to make it sing.

The way he manhandled me with such care.

I had no idea how incredible his brand of intimacy would make me feel, and now that I know, I'm not sure how to forget. Now I know what it's like to truly connect with someone on another level physically.

I've tried all morning to reassure myself he's not the only guy out there who knows how to make a woman scream. And that this sucky melancholy won't last forever. It doesn't do any good.

I feel like nothing will ever be okay again.

Dramatic?

Yes. Sue me.

Wrangling my turbulent emotions has been hard enough. The last thing I need is to tell the girls and have my spiraling doubts start from scratch.

What I fail to consider is the infallible intuition of a

bestie. When something is up with a soul sister, we know it in our guts. That's why Dani calls me and why I should have expected her call. Instead, I'm so lost in my own head that I startle and spill water all over myself before answering the phone.

"Hey, how's it going?" I try to sound normal, but my voice is deflated. Lifeless.

"I'm all good. I wanted to know about your night. How was it?"

"It was good. I danced a little, had champagne, then called it a night."

Silence.

"Why don't I believe you?"

Because you're my best friend, and you know me.

"It's nothing. I just have a bit of a stomachache this morning. Probably the champagne."

"Well, that sucks, but I'm glad you had a good time!"

"Yeah," I say wistfully. "What did you do last night?"

"I made Tommy watch *The Holiday* with me." Her grin is somehow audible over the phone and manages to lift my spirits a fraction.

"And is it his new favorite movie ever?" I ask playfully.

"Oh, definitely," she teases back. "Now, I have to watch *Die Hard* with him—that was the agreement."

"Ah, yes. The not-Christmassy Christmas movie."

"Indeed. Hey, before I forget, I also called to invite you to make Christmas cookies this afternoon at Amelie's place. She's baking now, so the cookies should be cooled and ready to decorate in a couple of hours."

"That's sweet of her!" I infuse as much enthusiasm in my voice as I can muster. It should come easily since I adore all things Christmas, but post-Dean, nothing has the same luster. "Does four o'clock work?"

"Yup. I told her Tommy and I would be around about that time, maybe a few minutes after."

"Sounds good. I'll see you then."

"Bye, babe."

"Bye."

I hang up and wonder when gravity in my apartment got so intense. I feel like I can hardly hold myself upright, and I need to find a cure before I go to Amelie's, or I'll be in for an interrogation. I considered using the fake stomachache as a reason to bow out of the decorating session, but the distraction will be good for me. The sooner I get back on that horse, the sooner I'll be ready to ride again.

My poorly chosen analogy brings to mind the vision of me straddling Dean.

His belt around my wrists.

The slap of his palm on my ass.

Lips like velvet tenderly kissing my temple.

Well, crap. Looks like it's time to cry again.

Cucumber slices have done wonders for my puffy eyes, but I'm sure Dani will still notice once she gets here. Amelie may have already noted it when I arrived, but she was too kind to bring it up if she did.

"I was just mixing the last of the icing colors," she says with a grin while I give her sweet dog a pet.

"Hey, Freya. You been a good girl?" I ask, wishing not for the first time that I had a dog or cat of my own. I lift my gaze back to Amelie and smile. "Thanks for doing this. The cookies smell delicious."

The intoxicating aroma of butter and sugar permeates the air in her beautiful apartment. The building is top-notch, and while her apartment is one of the smallest units, it's large for Manhattan standards. It was hers before she and Sante got married. The two have boatloads of money, so I wouldn't be surprised if they upgrade at some point, but her sister lives in the same building, so they've been content to stay.

"I'm just glad you could make it. I know this was last minute. The mood just struck, you know?"

"Absolutely, and I wasn't doing anything else, so this is perfect."

"Good. You get settled. I need to run to the restroom." She sweeps gracefully toward the hallway. Amelie does everything gracefully since she's a professional ballerina. She even sneezes gracefully.

Freya follows her. Where Amelie goes, Freya goes. They're pretty adorable.

I'm about to head to the kitchen to peek at the cookies when a knock sounds at the door. It's got to be Tommy and Dani. I spin back around and swing the door wide open, only to find Detective Dean Malone standing on the other side.

Time.

Stands.

Still.

He's here. At Amelie's apartment.

My shock is mirrored on his face. And what a beautiful face it is. He looks like a TikTok thirst trap in jeans and a snug cream-colored shirt, beneath a brown wool coat. And those eyes—they're even bluer in the daylight, making them all the more cutting when they narrow with thunderous rage.

"The fuck?"

10

Dean

For a split second, I ask myself if I'm hallucinating. Like maybe I've been thinking about Sachi so much that I tricked my eyes into seeing her. But, no, she's here in front of me, and she's just as shocked to see me as I am her. Not a happy sort of surprise. She's horrified.

That's when it hits me.

I'm at Sante's place.

She's somehow connected to him.

Did that motherfucker send a woman to seduce me? If so, I served myself up on a platter for her. Hell, I'm the one who invited her to my place.

I'm suddenly assaulted with questions. What the fuck did she do there while I was asleep? Was the entire night a performance? Are my instincts that far gone?

A whirlwind of thoughts and emotions comes at me all at once, building into a furious cyclone in an instant.

She starts to slam the door shut, but I manage to get a foot inside.

"I don't think so, *kitten*." I use my shoulder to pry open the door. "You're not getting rid of me that easily."

Sachi stumbles backward, her eyes wide and pretty pink lips parted. I should have made use of them last night when I had the chance. Now, I know she's more likely to bite my cock off than suck it. What a shame.

I nudge the door shut behind me, then cage her in against the entry wall. A part of me wants to shake her and demand answers, so I don't even tempt myself by touching her. That's not who I am. No matter how upset I get with a woman, I won't hurt her.

"What the hell are you doing here?" I demand, though the answer seems fairly obvious. "You work for Sante?"

"What? No! I'm friends with Amelie." Her stuttered explanation has little impact on my fury.

"Ah, so you going home with me last night and ending up here the following morning has nothing to do with Sante. It's all just a big coincidence."

"Yes."

"And you had no idea who I was," I continue for her, condescendingly.

"I ... I..."

"That's what I thought," I clip harshly. "Every bit of it was a lie, wasn't it?"

"No, I swear it wasn't a lie." Her wide eyes look so fucking innocent, and it pisses me off even more.

"You seriously expect me to believe that? I already checked the guest list, and guess what? You weren't on it." I lean in to growl the final words. At the same time, another growl sounds from behind me—this one much more animalistic.

Fuck.

Amelie's dog.

The German Shepherd is an expertly trained protection dog that will tear me to shreds if she decides I'm a threat. I gingerly turn my body to face the snarling beast, doing my best to cover Sachi because no matter how pissed I am, I don't want her getting hurt. Not like that. And I can tell she's terrified of the dog, her hands clutching the back of my jacket. I doubt she's ever seen the animal in attack mode—the change is impressive.

"Shh ... everything's okay. I'm not a danger to anyone." I say the words in the most reassuring tone possible, but it means nothing to the dog's trained responses.

"*Fuck*, where's Amelie?"

"Bathroom," Sachi whispers. She keeps her body close

to mine, and I hate how I still take enjoyment out of knowing I help her feel safe.

"Sachi? Freya?" Amelie rounds the corner into the living room, just out of our sight in the entry.

"Amelie, it's Malone. Please, call off your dog."

"What? Oh!" She finally approaches to see us pressed against the wall and takes hold of Freya's collar. She gives a single command in a foreign language that instantly calms the beast. "What on earth is going on?" she asks, turning her attention back to us.

Before I can answer, the front door opens as Sante, Tommy, and his wife join our little party. They go still as they take in the situation. Meanwhile, I see fucking red. I just know Sante is behind everything that happened last night, and I'm going to make him pay for it.

Catching him off guard, I shove him against the wall and hold him pinned with my hands fisted in his shirt.

"What the *fuck*, Malone?" He lifts his hands but doesn't fight back.

The girls all shriek, huddling together, and the dog returns to growling. Behind me, I hear the distinct click of the safety being disengaged on a handgun. Tommy's got a gun on me, but I'm too pissed to care.

"Who the *fuck* do you think you are sending someone to fuck with me?" I spit back at him.

Sante's face contorts as he gives me a wicked upper cut to the gut. My involuntary recoil allows him leeway to step away from me.

"Don't know what the fuck you're talking about, and you should fucking know better than to come into my house and start accusing me of shit."

The next thing I know, he's got a gun on me, too.

This situation is getting dangerously out of hand. If I don't walk away, someone's going to end up hurt ... or worse.

My eyes cut once more to Sachi, who looks on the verge of tears. That pisses me off all over again for a slew of reasons I don't want to analyze.

"I came by to tell you we got an address on Reaper. I know how important it is to you guys that we find that bastard. Here I am trying to be transparent, only to learn you're sending fucking spies rather than ask for whatever the fuck it is you think you were going to find. I know we don't exactly trust one another, but I thought we'd established some degree of professional respect. Turns out you wouldn't know how to be honorable if your pathetic life depended on it."

I'm walking a thin line. Sante's jaw is so tight he's thirty seconds from cracking a tooth. That's fine. I have nothing more to say to these people.

Fuck.

Them.

DEAN STORMS OUT, SLAMMING THE DOOR behind him.

The whole thing happens so fast, I can hardly wrap my head around it. I knew he wouldn't like knowing I was friends with Tommy and Sante. This was something else entirely. It never occurred to me he might think I'd been sent by them to steal ... what? Information? I'm too dumbfounded to even speculate.

Whatever conclusion he jumped to made him furious. And between my shock and the guys pointing guns, I never had a chance to correct him. Not that he would have believed me.

The image of his eyes bright with betrayal will haunt me forever.

I burst into tears.

"What the fuck is happening here?" Sante demands.

My sobs intensify as they all stare at me.

"It's my ... fault," I stutter between heaving breaths. "I should have said something."

I'm not even sure why I'm crying except the letdown of adrenaline. Between that and the culmination of my tormented emotions needing an outlet, I feel like my heart is spilling out on the floor all around me.

I take one shaky breath, then another.

Dani has her arms wrapped around me protectively. "Everything's okay, Sach. Promise. It's going to be okay."

I know I can count on her support, which makes me feel even worse for not telling her the truth about my night. Why do things always look so different in hindsight?

"I went home with Dean last night," I say on a whisper.

"Dean?" Tommy blurts.

"Malone, dickhead. She slept with Malone," Sante clarifies oh, so tactfully. "That's why he's so fucking upset. He thinks I sent her."

"I didn't tell him who I was, so he had no idea I was connected to you guys. I never expected to see him again, certainly not like this." I shake my head in shame. "I'm sorry I didn't say anything. I didn't want you guys to be upset or cause problems for you, but it looks like I did anyway."

"So that's why you sounded so off on the phone." Dani hugs me tighter. "Wait, you sounded kind of awful. She pulls back and studies my eyes. "He didn't do anything he wasn't supposed to, did he?"

My face crumples as I shake my head and dissolve into a new round of tears. "That's ... the problem," I force past the knot in my throat. "He did everything right. It was amazing," I rasp on a harsh exhale.

"Oh, honey." Amelie joins in on our hug. "That's not something to be upset about."

"It is," I explain to her. "How can I possibly be with a cop? I don't want to put you guys at risk. And it was just one night—it shouldn't have mattered." The last words are no more than a wisp of air as my voice fails me.

"You really liked him," Dani says with dawning realization.

"Yeah."

Silence hangs in the air like a thick fog.

"Come on, Tommy," Sante murmurs to his cousin. "Sounds like we have some things to discuss." The two head back to his office, leaving us girls to talk in private.

I watch them leave, my worries intensifying. "I've made a mess of things, haven't I?"

Amelie huffs. "No worse than they've done in the

past. They can sort things with Malone, no problem. I'm more worried about you."

"Definitely," Dani chimes in.

"I'll be fine. It was one stupid night, right? It shouldn't mean anything."

Amelie sweeps a lock of hair behind my ear and smiles softly. "If Sante has taught me anything, it's that following standards set by other people will only set you up for disappointment. Whatever you two shared last night, it clearly meant a lot to both of you, regardless of what should or shouldn't be."

"You really think so?"

"I do. I've never seen Malone so upset. I was completely stunned. Those guys do stuff to piss him off all the time, but it's like water off a duck's back. The accusation was pretty egregious, but his anger was personal. He did *not* like thinking you used him."

My chin quivers despite her reassurance. "He hates me so much, now."

Dani waves a hand. "Men are emotional like that. Once he gets the whole story, he'll come around."

I shake my head. "If he lets himself hear it, and even then, it doesn't change the fact that we move in very different circles."

"It might not be easy, but only time will tell. Don't write him off yet." Amelie's lips pull into a thin, sorrowful smile. "I know you may not be in the mood, but we still have loads of cookies to decorate. It might make you feel better." She peers at me questioningly.

She's right. I'm not really in the mood, but what else am I going to do? Go back home and be depressed? Tempting, but I probably shouldn't. I'll get past this whole ordeal much faster if I keep busy. That's why I came over in the first place, right?

I nod. "Yeah, let's decorate some cookies." It can't make me feel any worse.

We spend two hours talking and designing cookies in the shape of ball ornaments, presents, and stockings. My time with them truly is cathartic. They keep the topics of conversation light, and by the time I'm packing up to go home, my emotional storm has ebbed, leaving me calm but exhausted. Hopefully, a good night's rest will bring a more positive perspective in the morning.

"I'll drive you home," Sante offers, grabbing his keys from the entry table.

"You sure? I have no problem walking."

"Yeah, I don't think Malone would corner you, but he was pretty upset. I'd feel better making sure you got home safely."

"Okay. Thank you."

I can't imagine Dean hurting me, but having Sante with me won't hurt, so I don't argue. Once we're in the car, I realize Sante's gesture had little to do with Dean's anger and more to do with his desire to have a few words with me alone.

"I appreciate that you want to look out for us, but you don't have to do that. We aren't afraid of the cops."

I nod, gnawing on the inside of my cheek. "I'm glad, but it worries me that if I dated someone like Dean, you guys wouldn't want Amelie and Dani to be around me as much. They mean the world to me—all of you guys do—I don't want to risk losing that."

"One, you don't even know if it would work out between you, and two, Malone isn't gonna get shit on us."

I flash a small smile because what he's doing is sweet.

"Mellie tell you to talk to me?"

"Yeah, but despite what she may think, I don't have to listen to her. I'm talking to you as myself. I don't understand the draw to Officer Hotshot, but if that's what does it for you, then have at it."

"It's *Detective* Hotshot," I tease softly.

He cuts a glance my direction, his lips hooked upward in a wry smirk.

"Whatever."

The first genuine grin of the day spreads across my lips and warms my heart. However, while getting his permission is sweet, I don't think it changes anything. Dean thinks the absolute worst of me right now. Even if I explain what happened, it won't undo the harm, but I appreciate knowing Sante would support me if things somehow worked out.

We park outside my building, and Sante even walks me to my apartment door.

"Try not to let him upset you, Sach. Everything will work out for the best. You'll see." He taps my chin like a big brother might, and my heart swells.

Sante, Amelie, Tommy, and Dani are the family I never knew I needed. And while I may be the fifth wheel, they only ever make me feel wanted. I'm absolutely right in prioritizing my relationship with them over that of an unlikely romance. I know it's true. So why do I feel like I have a boa constrictor squeezing so tight around my rib cage that I can't breathe?

"Thanks, Sante," I manage to get past my tight throat. "I really appreciate you bringing me home and everything you've said."

He shrugs. "Not that Malone would try anything crazy—he's too straight-laced for that—but it never hurts to be safe."

I give him a weak smile and enter the code to unlock my door. "See ya."

He waves and turns back toward the elevator. I take a step inside my dark apartment when a hand clamps tightly over my mouth, and I'm yanked inside, the door closing behind me.

I suck in air through my nose to attempt a muffled scream only to have an all-too-familiar scent invade my lungs.

Dean.

He's here.

I freeze.

In my shock, I have a second to take in the feel of his large frame behind me. I'm pulled flush against his front, one of his strong arms wrapped around my torso to keep me in place. I should be terrified, and for a moment, I was. But now that I know who's behind me, an odd sense of relief washes over me until Dean finally speaks, and his words chill me to the bone.

"Wouldn't try anything crazy, huh? Apparently, Sante doesn't know me as well as he thinks he does."

12

Dean

I was going to claw Sachi from my memory. That's what I decided on my ride in the elevator after leaving Amelie's apartment. Because as much as her actions felt like a betrayal, there was nothing to betray. Sachi never owed me anything. It's Sante who deserves my wrath.

With each step I take toward the building exit, I try to convince myself that Sachi means nothing to me, and thus, I shouldn't spend another minute thinking of her.

I try really damn hard.

Turns out, I'm even more persistent than I gave myself

credit for being. I know I need to walk away from Sachi, but I can't do it. I need to know why. I need to understand how she could have been so fucking convincing when it was all a fucking act. If I don't get to the bottom of it, doubts about my intuition will haunt me forever.

Therefore, instead of taking a long walk to cool off before going home, I never make it past the building's lobby. I use my credentials to get Sachi's full name from building security, then locate her apartment using an official police database.

Next thing I know, I'm breaking into the damn place.

I had sensed from the moment I laid eyes on Sachi that she had the potential to inspire great and terrible things in me. It's good to know my instincts haven't totally failed me.

I haven't done anything irreversible yet, but that may change when she walks through this door. I'm not certain what I'll do. I just know I never would have thought myself capable of any of this before Sachi.

I've sat here in her apartment for the last thirty minutes looking at her ridiculous abundance of Christmas decorations while I consider just how far I'm willing to take this. Her place is tiny, as are most Manhattan apartments, but she has every square inch decked out in festive decorations. She even has a six-foot tree halved from the top to the bottom so it sits flush against the wall. Nothing else would have fit in here, but she made it work. She has fake snow sprayed on her windows, additional lights lining the ceiling edge, and every other bit of red and green decor imaginable.

The woman really goes all out for the holidays—not exactly what I'd expect from someone willing to fuck me for information, but clearly, I'm no longer a decent judge of character.

When she finally arrives home, I hear multiple voices in the hallway. Her studio apartment doesn't offer a wide array of hiding places, so I stand flush against the wall next to the door.

I register Sante's voice.

A renewed fury has my fists balling.

This could get really fucking ugly if he comes in here because despite what he thinks, I'm not above beating the shit out of him. Not anymore. The minute Sachi stormed into my life, the rules changed, whether I wanted them to or not. I'm not even sure I know what the rules are where she's concerned. I just know I'm pissed, and she's going to answer for what she's done.

I don't waste any time. The second Sachi is within reach, I grab her and shut the door.

She stiffens with panic.

She should.

I'm three times her size in mass. Subduing her takes no effort at all. I'm not even worried when she sucks in air to scream, except the sound never comes. Time stretches thin before she releases the breath, and her body softens in my hold.

She knows who has her, and the knowledge innately relaxed her.

Fuck, I hate how good that feels.

Not that she should feel safe right now. *I* don't even know what I might do next.

"Wouldn't try anything crazy, huh?" I mull over what I heard. "Apparently, Sante doesn't know me as well as he thinks he does."

Not that I'll actually hurt her. I might put a fist through the wall, but I'd never lay a hand on her. I'm just so damn frustrated. I thought she and I had truly connected. That we had a magnetic chemistry neither of us could resist.

Turned out, I had just seen what I wanted to see.

Turned out, I'd been played.

I spin us around so that her back is against the wall with me facing her. I keep one hand across her mouth and use the other to pin her hands above her head.

"I'm going to remove my hand, and you're not going to scream. Understood?"

She nods.

I ease my hand away. It slides down to her throat and angles her face so her eyes are lifted to mine.

"What were you after?" My voice is sharp as a blade and equally ruthless.

She shakes her head. "Nothing. Sante and Tommy had nothing to do with this, I swear."

"You must think I'm real fucking dumb," I growl at her.

She lets out a whimper, and I have to fight back the urge to apologize for Christ knows what.

"You weren't on that guest list. You hid the fact that you were in with the Morettis. You fucking lied, Sachi. Now, tell me why, *goddammit*." My outburst causes me to accidentally tighten my grip. Sachi's eyes widen a fraction, but she doesn't struggle, despite the fear reflected in those beautiful brown eyes.

I instantly relax my hold.

I can't help it. Despite it all, I don't want to hurt her. I don't even want her to fear me, though that's the only way I'm going to find out what this was all about.

"I did lie to you, but not in the way you're thinking." Her softly spoken confession is calm. Vulnerable. I sense genuine grief, and I don't understand it. My intuition has never failed me on such a grand scale. But if I were to believe what my gut is telling me, how can I possibly align that with everything I've learned?

"You were horrified to see me on the other side of that door," I remind her *and* myself.

"Yes, because I was worried my friends would be upset and that you'd hate me for deceiving you."

"You're saying they didn't know you were there."

"They knew I went, but they knew nothing about you."

"And why, pray tell, did they think you were at the

ball?" My question drips condescension because I can't imagine how she can explain her way out of this.

"I wasn't on the guest list, but I didn't sneak in," she whispers, her gaze dropping as though in ... what? Embarrassment? What would she have to be embarrassed about? I stay quiet and allow her to continue. "I was there for work. I was part of the catering team."

My body stills as I process what she's told me.

I hadn't even considered that possibility, mostly because there hasn't been enough time, and I've been too worked up to think clearly during the time I *have* had. "You were supposed to be a server at the party?"

"No, I'm a sculptor. I carved the fruit displays."

I think back to the food tables. "Poinsettias."

She nods.

"The art gallery," I recall. "You said you started out in sculpting."

"There is a gallery, but I work there. I don't own it."

"I don't understand," I demand impatiently. Why all the smoke and mirrors? What's the motive?

Her chin quivers, cinching a vise tight around my chest. "I work all these extravagant parties, and for once, I just wanted to experience things from the other side. One night of indulgence. I never expected the rest to happen."

I chew on her words and hunt for the telltale tang of deception. "You weren't surprised when you saw me tonight—not the same way I was. You knew who I was." It's the one sticking point I have left. I've never met her, but she somehow knew me. She knew seeing me at Sante's place was a possibility.

"Months ago, Sante gave me a ride home, and he met up with you on the way. I stayed in the car, but I saw you two talking. I knew you were a cop and that you two knew each other. That's it, I swear."

Fuck, I want to believe her.

What the hell is wrong with me? Am I really going to buy this hook, line, and sinker?

My hand clenches tighter as I battle indecision. It's not enough to leave a mark, but I can tell she's uncomfortable, though she's trying to be brave.

My sweet, brave girl.

I stare into her wide, mournful eyes—eyes glassy with unshed tears—and I begin to drown in their depths. And that's exactly where I want to be. That's how I know I've lost this fight. I'd rather sink in her sorrows than drag myself ashore all alone.

"What the fuck are you doing to me?" I barely get the words out before my lips crash down on hers.

13

Sachi

RELIEF SWEEPS IN LIKE A TIDAL WAVE AND CARRIES me away. To feel Dean's touch again—and not out of anger but desire—gives me a world of hope, and I seize it with both hands.

He does the same.

Our frenzied fingers claw at one another, ripping off clothes and clinging to contact. I fist my hand in his hair. He kisses a ravenous path down my throat. I lift my shirt off over my head. He does the same. I lave my tongue over one of his tight little nipples. He fists my hair with a gentle tug and commands my gaze to his.

"Tell me I'm not imagining this."

The desperation in his plea is a knife to my gut. I feel wretched that I made him question himself and everything we shared. I don't know if we have true long-term potential or not, but this insane chemistry is very real.

"It's not just you. I feel it, too."

When his lips return to mine, a part of my soul takes flight.

"I need to fuck you again," he rasps, nipping at my bottom lip.

"Yes, *please.*"

Our clothes are off in a heartbeat. Dean sheathes himself in a condom, then lifts me in his arms, pressing my back against the wall. I arch at the shock of the cold on my skin. He takes the opportunity to suck my breast into his warm mouth. The two competing sensations have my insides clenching tight with need.

I moan wantonly.

Dean doesn't make me wait.

He aligns himself at my entrance, then surges inside me in two swift thrusts. If my arousal wasn't already dripping from me, the sudden intrusion would have been painful, but that's not a problem where Dean is concerned. My body welcomes him with open arms. And it's a good thing, because he doesn't stop there.

Dean fucks me against the wall with ruthless abandon.

Hammering into me, over and over.

I don't know if this is a reward or a punishment, but

I'll happily take it either way. I've never come from pene-tration alone, but the intensity of this situation has me unraveling at the seams. When his mouth latches onto my breast, and his teeth graze over my nipple, I explode.

My cries echo off the walls.

As elation illuminates my body from the inside out, it's all I can do to cling to his shoulders as he continues in pursuit of his own release. And when he bellows with satisfaction, my heart blooms brighter than a field of wild-flowers. But just as quickly, the darkness creeps in around us.

Renewed uncertainty whispers between our rapid breaths.

Dean carries me to the bathroom the same as he did last night, though the walk is much shorter in my place. He wets a washcloth with warm water and tenderly cleans me. Only after he's satisfied that I'm taken care of does he remove the condom and wash himself.

The whole time, hardly a word is spoken.

The silence screams louder in my head than any words ever could. I don't understand it. I get that this is all new, but I thought we established I never meant to deceive him.

Unless ... he doesn't believe me.

He wouldn't have sex with me again if he doubted me, would he? I hate to think so, but I am so out of my depth. I have no idea what is going on in his head.

I don't want to push him, yet I can't leave things like this, so once he's dressed, I offer the only thing left to say.

"Dean?" I wait for him to meet my gaze. "I'm so sorry." For deceiving him. For putting us both in an impossibly tricky situation. And for being incapable of resisting him. I hope he knows that I never meant to harm anyone.

"If everything you've said tonight is true, there's no need to be sorry." His unreadable gaze sweeps over me one last time before he gives a single nod and leaves.

14

Dean

I CAN'T CONCENTRATE TO SAVE MY LIFE. AND THERE *are* lives at stake. It's Monday, I'm back at the station, and I should be coordinating surveillance ops so we can get our hands on The Reaper, but all I can think about is that last heartbroken look Sachi gave me when I walked out her door.

Fuck.

Me.

I left because I needed space to think through everything. Any reassurances I could have given on my way out would have been empty because I had no fucking clue what I was going to do about Sachi. A night of obsessing over it hasn't helped, either. I'm still just as torn.

She affects me in ways I don't like, but that shit's on me. It's not her fault I turn into a raving lunatic around her.

If she's telling the truth, she's done nothing wrong.

Except for a poor choice of friends.

A part of me is desperate to have her, regardless of who her friends are. She isn't her friends, after all. And maybe things with Sachi won't even work out. I won't know unless I give it a chance. If she is the perfect woman for me, am I willing to reject her over her friends?

No. It's that simple.

She likes them for the same reason I'm willing to cooperate with them—despite their shady morals, Sante and Tommy are halfway decent human beings.

When I step back and take it all in, I have to ask myself, what's the problem?

If I can confirm Sachi isn't lying to me, and her friends aren't a deal-breaker, why the indecision?

A single word whispers through my mind, causing me to cringe.

Pride.

Is that seriously my only hang-up?

That's how it's looking, but I'm not certain. It's hard to tell if my wariness is rooted in rational reasoning or a wounded ego. Something is holding me back. One thing I can say for sure is that life would be less complicated without linking myself to the Moretti crime family.

My thoughts are interrupted by the desk phone ringing with a call from reception.

"Malone," I answer.

"A man is waiting for you outside, told me to tell you his name was … *Santa*." The word is spoken with a wealth of exasperation. "I know it's the holidays, but come on."

The eclectic variety of informants we deal with often uses pseudonyms. It seems one of them is feeling especially festive today. "I'm on it, thanks."

I hang up and take a deep, weary breath before heading to the front of the station. Half of the time, the type of individuals in the business of information spook and disappear before I show up. I'm prepared to turn around and walk right back inside when I see a familiar face scowling at me.

Reception got it wrong.

Sante has paid me a visit, not Santa. Now, I'm even more on guard.

"What's up?" I ask, giving him a curt nod.

We both lean against the exterior stone wall, our bodies facing the street as though we're only casually aware of one another.

"I know you like to think the worst of me, but you need to know I didn't send her."

"So I hear."

"Yeah, well. I wouldn't bother correcting your assumption, but our working relationship has been mutually beneficial, and I don't see any reason this should disrupt things." His gaze slowly slides my direction. "You talk to her?"

"Last night." I nod.

"Not sure if you know this, but she's Tommy's wife's best friend."

"And?" Impatience and a touch of irritation sharpen my tone.

He shrugs a shoulder. "Figure it's good to point out how monumentally stupid it would be to fuck around and hurt her."

"That a threat?" I look over at him, wanting him to meet my steely stare and understand he can't scare me. He's pissing me off, more than anything.

"It's a fact, that's all." He pushes off the wall and stretches his neck. "The whole point is, it was purely an accident your paths crossed. Think it's best for everyone if we pretend it never happened." He gives me a pointed look, then walks away.

I envision myself yanking him back around and planting my fist in his face. The same fist I have balled so tightly my bones ache.

Why the fuck am I so pissed about what he said?

It's true. I was already telling myself the same thing, but coming from him, I hate it even more.

I stare poison-coated daggers at his back, not going

inside until he disappears around a corner two blocks down.

I'll be damned if I'm going to let that asshole dictate who I can and can't see.

I spend an hour trying to work. It's no use. I still can't concentrate, which is how I find myself on the phone with the catering company the city used to host our masquerade ball. Once I confirm Sachi didn't lie about working for them, I look her up on social media because she's a mystery, and it's my job to solve mysteries. Also, because I'm a glutton for punishment.

I didn't pay a whole lot of attention to the food at the party. The photos she's posted jog my memory, and I'm beyond impressed. The woman has some serious talent. And not just sculpting fruit—she works with all sorts of sculpting mediums, and they're all equally as spectacular.

Double fuck.

It's looking more and more like my assumptions about Sachi were a catastrophic jump to conclusions. And on top of that, I was an absolute dick about it. Hell, I fucked her against the wall, then walked out like she was some sort of cheap toy.

Before I know what I'm doing, I've taken the tennis ball that sits on my desk and thrown it as hard as I can at a metal filing cabinet. The ball dents the gray metal, then ricochets into a half-full can of soda on my desk, sending the can and its contents spilling to the floor.

Motherfucking goddammit.

Today is really starting to piss me off.

And things only go downhill from there. After problems arise in our Reaper stakeout, and a fucking pigeon shits on me on my way back from lunch, I decide this day literally can't get any worse.

Another erroneous assumption.

Midafternoon, Amelie pays me a visit. Ordinarily, I'd appreciate a chance to see her. She's warm and funny and an all-around good person. She's the reason I first crossed paths with Sante, her husband—though, he wasn't her husband at the time. He was her stalker.

It was complicated.

Now, Amelie and I are casual friends. I don't think Sante would allow much more. Seeing her would be a happy surprise if I didn't already know the reason for her visit.

"You and your husband in one day, I must be extra lucky." Is that sarcasm in my voice? 100 percent. Does it earn me a raised brow warning? Absolutely.

Amelie may be sweet, but she doesn't put up with crap. That's why I like her and respect her opinion, and why I really don't want to hear about what an asshole I've been.

"Have a seat," I say defeatedly.

"Thanks, I won't keep you long."

My lips thin. "Sorry about last night. Didn't mean to cause a scene."

"It happens. I've been the center of a little drama here

and there." She smirks playfully, lightening the mood and easing the tension in my shoulders.

"If you're here to tell me all the ways I've fucked up, then you can save your breath. I'm aware."

"That's good to hear, but not exactly why I came."

I motion for her to continue.

"I've gotten to know Sachi really well in the past few months, and she's one of the most genuine, decent people I've ever met." Amelie smiles softly at me. "She's a lot like you in that way."

And ... there it is. Cue the guilt.

"I wouldn't stick my nose in where it doesn't belong if I hadn't seen for myself how upset she was last night after you left my apartment. She feels really awful about what happened, and after thinking about how upset you were, as well, I think there's a solid chance you were into her just as much as she was into you. I hate for a misunderstanding to come between you before anything ever has a chance to begin."

"I appreciate you wanting to help, but it may be a little late for that." My grimace deepens with every word.

"That's your call to make. I certainly can't tell you whether the risk is worth it, but I'll be cheering for you guys." Amelie stands, righting her purse strap on her shoulder and smiling. "That's really all I wanted to say, so I'll let you get back to work."

I stand. "Amelie?"

She pauses, smiling over her shoulder at me. "Yeah?"

"Thanks, not that I deserve it."

"Hey, the situation was complicated. Anyone else would have reacted the same as you did. The question now is, what are you going to do about it?" She gives one last smile, then glides with her ballerina grace from my office, leaving me to ponder the million-dollar question.

What *am* I going to do about Sachi?

15

Sachi

P RETENDING WAS SUPPOSED TO BE A FUN DEPARTURE
from the humdrum parts of a life I otherwise enjoy. I
wanted the equivalent of a weekend getaway and effectively moved into a yurt in the middle of Montana.
Nothing against Montana. It's just not where I'd hoped
to be.

A bleak sense of melancholy was *not* the goal.

Things I normally enjoy have lost their luster. And
the kicker is, I'm still me, living in the city of my dreams.
Nothing has truly changed except the way I feel. Ever
since Dean Malone swept himself into my life, some-

thing inside me has shifted, and I'm not sure I can shift it back.

A weighted blanket of disappointment is draped over my shoulders, making every move feel cumbersome.

I know I'll get over it. I hardly knew the man, after all. It was two nights of mind-blowing sex. That's it. Of course, the dancing was really nice.

And our flirtatious banter at the ball had me feeling more giddy than I have in ages.

And then there was the tender way he held me when we went to sleep the first night…

The scent of his yummy aftershave.

The way he rescued me from those creeps.

He called me kitten…

Okay, so it was only two encounters, but they were jam-packed with a thousand scrumptious tidbits, and now, he's gone. It's no wonder I feel like hiding in a hole.

It's been a week, Sach. Time to shake it off.

A full week, and no word from him. I have to assume it's over and move on.

My phone buzzes with a call, and my emotions take a dizzying leap of hope, only to plummet when I see it's the manager of the catering company I work with. I stare at the screen and debate whether to answer. I don't want to. I don't want to do anything, but I need to take the call if I'm going to claw my way out of this pit of despair.

I sigh wearily and tap the green accept button.

"Hey, Shelly. What's up?"

"We've got a last-minute request for Saturday evening —it's a holiday donors' appreciation dinner for some kids' charity. Black tie. One hundred guests. I know you said you didn't want to work that day, but everyone else is booked up, and they were super excited about this. Someone from the police ball saw your work and asked for you specifically."

Oh ... well, that's always nice to hear. And it's a small event ... for kids. The black-tie part doesn't really affect me. I usually set up my contribution, then head out, but I like to know that sort of thing to make sure my designs are suitable for the theme.

"What are they wanting?" I've learned the hard way to always ask this crucial question before agreeing to an event.

"The charity logo carved in a watermelon and some kind of festive border. I'll text you the logo. Hang on."

I put her on speaker and pull up my messages. While I wait, I tell myself I need to take this job. Aside from needing the money, this would be a perfect distraction. It's the last Saturday before Christmas. The final event of the season. I had kept the day open on my schedule when my parents had mentioned possibly coming out to visit, but that fell through. I have absolutely no reason not to work this event.

The image from Shelly pops up on my screen. It's simple—the imprint of a small child's hand within the larger outline of an adult hand—and it's so sweet that the sight tugs at my heartstrings.

"Yeah, I can do that. Send me the details."

"Thank you so much, Sachi! I really appreciate it."

"No problem. If I don't see you, have a Merry Christmas."

"You, too!"

I close my phone and look around my dark apartment with a tiny seed of hope sprouting in my chest. Usually, I'd have all the multicolored lights glowing bright in my capsule apartment, but they simply felt too cheery. It's been two days since I had them on—something that's entirely out of character for me. The old me never would have wasted a second of the holiday season.

It's time to make a change.

I pick up the small remote for my tree lights and click them on. The strands around the ceiling and windows are still off. I'm not ready for full-scale joy.

My wall-mounted half tree twinkles with a rainbow of color.

I adore the holiday season, and in less than a week, Christmas will be over. I don't want to ignore the good in my life because of one disappointment. My short connection with Dean is a good reminder to appreciate what I have while I have it because life is always changing. Today, I have a cozy place in the heart of the city, pursuing a career I adore, with friends who love me. That's plenty for me, and who knows what tomorrow may bring.

16

Dean

I lost my parents when I was sixteen years old. If there was any sort of silver lining to their loss, it was my ability to appreciate things that most young people take for granted. Things like my dad fussing about my grades or my mom wanting to know every little detail about where I would be hanging out with friends on a Friday night.

That stuff can seem like a hassle until it's gone.

After the loss of my parents, I would have given anything to be grounded or get a lecture—anything if it meant having them back. Since that wasn't possible, I tried to honor their teachings as best I could.

Something my mother always preached was righting a mistake. She used to tell me that everyone messes up, and while we shouldn't be too hard on ourselves, we also have an obligation to do what we can to atone. Often, that's as simple as an apology. Sometimes corrective actions are needed. Either way, it's important to own our mistakes and do what we can to fix them.

I screwed up with Sachi. Big time.

That is not up for debate.

I just hope my attempt to right the situation doesn't blow up in my face because I've decided to combine my apology with a do-over. I could have gone to her place, told her I was sorry about everything, then left her alone, but I didn't like that option. It didn't feel like enough. I don't want to simply smooth things over; I want another chance, and I need to earn it. When I considered the best way to go about it, I decided it would be best to go back to the beginning.

Two people unexpectedly crossing paths at a party.

Instead of the Waldorf, we're at Le Jardinier—a lovely event space decked out for a formal dinner. The charity event has been in the works for months and felt like the perfect opportunity. The event may not have been arranged for her, but tonight will be all about her in every other way possible.

I'm in my tux—the same one I wore a week ago to the masquerade. Sachi is wearing the simple all-black uniform of the catering staff as she sets up her intricate carving display. The other guests have yet to arrive. So far, everything is going to plan, but what happens next is unscripted because Sachi has no idea that I'm here.

She's about to find out.

She'll learn my plans for the evening and so much more because I'm not the ordinary detective she thought I was. I've decided to make a play for her, and that means telling her everything. I'm going to lay all my cards on the table.

Using the party as a means for my unveiling made sense in my head, but I have no idea how I'll be received. This could be the best decision I've ever made or an absolute disaster. Only time will tell which it will be, and that time is now.

17

Sachi

"THEY CHANGED THE SEATING CHART AT THE LAST minute." The head caterer holds up a map of the place settings with a scowl.

"You need help sorting it out?" I do a visual sweep of the seven dining tables decked out with gorgeous live floral arrangements—all festive in an elegant, sophisticated fashion. Sprigs of pine fill the room with their evergreen scent alongside holly and eucalyptus leaves, providing an artful background for spectacular crimson peonies and bright red berries. Each set of fine China is adorned with a placard bearing a guest's name, beautifully inscribed in calligraphy.

"Hey, this is funny." The older woman holds up one of the tented placards. "I've never met another Sachi."

"Me either," I muse. "Of course, I've never lived in Japan. I have no idea how popular the name is over there."

"True." She swaps out the old card for the new one, then moves to another table. "You know what it means?"

"My name? It means happiness or good fortune." I smile softly, thinking of my parents and how they swore my name would guide me to a fulfilling life. I don't always understand their way of thinking, but they're still great parents. They love me with their whole hearts.

"I like that. More interesting than mine," she grumbles, making another card swap. "Okay, I think that does it." She lifts her gaze and smiles at me. "You heading out?"

"Yeah, unless you need me?"

Please, say no.

"Nah, we should be fine."

"Kay, I'll see you after Christmas, then!"

"Have a good one!"

"You, too." I give her a wave with a smile, then turn for the exit and discover we're not alone. And it's not just anyone watching us; it's Dean. He's dressed in that impeccable black velvet tux he wore to the masquerade. "What are you doing here?" I ask in a hushed tone, peering around to see if the head caterer has noticed him. Bringing drama to my friend group is enough. I don't want my personal life bleeding into work as well, and I can't fathom why else he'd be here except to talk about things better discussed in private. Why he came in a tux to talk, I have no idea. And how did he find me?

My whole body tenses from the uncertainty of the situation.

"Preparing for dinner, same as you," he offers in that honeyed voice of his.

I peer back at the tables, as if they'll provide clarity. "Dinner?" I'm so freaking confused.

"Yeah, I'm on the board of trustees for the charity, so technically, I'm one of the hosts."

I take him in again, this time in a new light. "You're here for the event, not me." I hate how pathetic the words sound as they tumble past my lips, and I wish I could gobble them back inside.

"There is only one reason I'm here." Dean ambles forward, slowly closing the distance between us. "And that has everything to do with you." He cups my face with his large hands and leans in to whisper close to my ear. "I'm sorry, Sachi, for how I responded, and I'm really hoping you'll give me another chance."

I lift my wide eyes to his imploring gaze and lose myself for a second in their sapphire depths.

"You knew I'd be here? You're the one who requested me?" I say my thoughts aloud as understanding dawns. How else would he have known I'd be here at an event he happened to be hosting? An event where I was specifically requested. Days ago. He'd been planning this for days.

He bites his bottom lip in a sheepishly boyish way that has my heart melting into a puddle at my feet.

"I know it's unexpected. I could have just come to talk to you or called, but that didn't feel like enough. A major fuckup deserves an epic apology."

"I'm not sure I understand, but we can probably talk tomorrow after the dinner," I respond, confusion furrowing my brows.

"Oh, no. This apology is all about you, and it starts right now." He takes my hand and guides me down a hallway and into a sitting room. Inside is a clothing rack lined with beautiful cocktail gowns. "I'd be honored if you'd be my guest for dinner tonight."

My jaw drops.

"Those are dresses." My gears are a little slow to catch up.

"Yes," he says with a note of amusement.

"And that was my name." I point absently over my shoulder toward the banquet room. "On the placard."

"Yes, again."

"You want me to put on a dress and join you for dinner at your charity banquet."

His beaming grin heats the room a solid ten degrees with its radiance. "Exactly."

I place my hands on my head and try to recall the state of my hair. "I don't have a brush."

I swear to God, the most inane things keep coming out of my mouth, but I can't help it. I'm utterly flabbergasted.

Dean takes my hands in his, his expression sobering. "The people attending dinner tonight are all incredibly generous, gracious people. I wouldn't think you'd have anything to worry about, but just to make sure you're comfortable, I have a hair and makeup stylist waiting in another room. I understand this is a big ask with no warning, so it's totally up to you. The dress, shoes, and jewelry are all available for your selection, but if you'd rather not, I'll respect your decision."

Jewelry? A stylist?

He's put a ton of thought and planning into tonight.

Aside from still being in shock, I'm flattered and incredibly grateful.

Excitement pulls my lips into a wide grin and brings creases to the corners of my smiling eyes. "Do I pick any dress I want?"

He flashes his sexy dimples, fighting a grin. "Take your pick."

I slide the hangers down and have a look at each gown one at a time. It's not an easy choice. "They're all so gorgeous." So much so that I run my hands down one looking for a tag. I don't recognize the label, nor can I find a price tag, but I can tell by the quality that the dresses must cost a small fortune.

"Something wrong?" Dean asks, his tone wary.

"No, I'm just a little confused. Where did you get these?"

"A boutique shop where a friend works."

"They just agreed to loan you dresses for the night?" If I'd known that was an option, I would have done that for every party ever.

"No, the dresses are yours. Bought and paid for."

I freeze, turning a wide-eyed stare up at the beautiful man standing beside me. The New York City detective, who most likely would have to cash in his pension to buy one of these dresses, let alone all of them. "Dean, it's too much," I whisper, praying we can get his money back.

His lips twist as he considers his response. Meanwhile, my heart pounds in my chest like a war drum.

"This always gets a little awkward to admit." He brings a hand sheepishly to the back of his neck. "I'm a detective—you know that—but what you and most people don't know is my parents were killed in a hit-and-run accident when I was sixteen."

My stomach lurches as a horrified chill brings goose bumps to my arms.

"I spent the next couple of years fostered by a relative until I was an adult and had access to my inheritance, which was ... sizable."

"Your apartment," I breathe, the pieces clicking into place.

Dean nods. "I figured you probably noticed."

"It's huge ... and really, *really* nice."

"I definitely couldn't have bought that on my salary alone."

I take a renewed look at the man opposite me. His tux is perfection—luxury fabrics tailored with precision. He's hosting a charity banquet. He has the equivalent of a mansion apartment in the heart of the city.

"Are you ... *rich?*"

A rumble of masculine amusement tickles my ears as he places his hands on either side of my face and brings his lips to my forehead.

"I wish you could see your face right now."

"Dean Malone, are you making fun of me?" I jab at him lightheartedly.

"Maybe just a tiny bit," he says, bringing his eyes to mine. "But only because you're adorable."

His touch and smell and stare are wreaking delicious havoc on my senses, scrambling my thoughts, but not enough that I lose sight of what's important.

"You have money, but only because you lost your parents," I say softly, gently. My heart bleeds silent tears for the pain he must have endured. I can't even imagine.

He sobers. "I'd give it all up in an instant if it meant getting them back, but that's not how it works."

"Instead, you became a cop."

He gives a single nod.

"You don't need to work, but you don't see it as just a job, do you?" I recall the guys describing dean as a Goody

Two-Shoes. Now I understand why. He's not the type who can be bought ... at any price.

"Being on the force is a choice. I've been somewhat righteous about that in the past, but I've come to understand that life isn't always black and white. Having money makes it easy for me to stay on the right side of the law—a luxury most others aren't afforded—and something I took for granted until this breathtaking beauty captivated me at a party." His voice lowers to a gravelly rasp as he takes my hands in his and walks me backward until my legs bump against the back of a chair.

"You broke into my apartment," I remind him softly.

He weaves his fingers through mine and brings his lips to my jawline, grazing his teeth against my skin. "I also used official resources to get your information. I honestly can't say just how far I'd bend the law if it meant getting a second chance with you." He withdraws, his gaze seizing mine. "Spend the evening with me, Sachi. Have dinner as my guest—no other expectations—just you and me and conversation."

He wants a do-over. Dean Malone gave me a fancy party to attend, just like I'd wanted. He's provided everything I could need, including his remorse over what transpired between us, and all he's asking for in return is an opportunity to make things right.

How can I possibly say no?

He has me utterly spellbound.

"I'll take the red dress, please."

I WAIT FOR SACHI FOR WHAT FEELS LIKE AN ETERNITY. In reality, it's not long at all, but every drawn-out second etches away at my nerves. I steal repeated glances toward the doorway where Sachi will appear—something that could easily come off as rude, considering I'm also in the middle of talking to important donor guests.

It's important that they feel appreciated.

Their money is *very* appreciated, and I'd like to keep it flowing.

My distracted obsession with the opposite end of the room isn't a great look, but I can't help it. I have an irrational fear that if I don't lay eyes on Sachi soon, she might disappear—totally ridiculous considering there's no exit down that hallway. My brain doesn't care. It worries that she'll find a way out, and I'll lose her forever.

I do my best to suppress my fears and exchange pleasantries with a few new arrivals. When the moment does finally arrive, and Sachi rounds that corner, the excruciating wait is instantly forgotten. I'm literally winded by her beauty, especially the radiant smile that lights her face the instant our eyes meet.

Fuck, this woman pulls strings in me I didn't know existed.

I excuse myself from the older woman I'm visiting with and go to Sachi.

"If you were any more stunning, I'd worry for the cardiac safety of the elderly men in this room."

Sachi drops her gaze as she gives a small laugh. "I suppose it's good I didn't let the stylist spend overly long on my hair and makeup."

"Your sacrifice has saved lives, madam." I give her a playful, pointed look, then lean in close and whisper, "In all seriousness, Sachi, you are absolutely ravishing." I place an earnest kiss on her cheek. "Thank you."

"For what?" she asks in a breathless whisper.

"For hearing me out. For the opportunity to earn a second chance. I made some horrible assumptions about you, and my behavior was an embarrassment. You'd be justified in refusing to give me the time of day, but I'm grateful that's not the case, and I promise to do everything in my power to redeem myself."

Sachi nods. I get the sense she's choked up and pray it's a good thing. I've said my piece, and now it's time to follow through.

I step to her side and rest my hand at the base of her spine. "Shall we grab some champagne and take a seat?"

"That sounds perfect."

The thing about Sachi is, when she smiles, she radiates joy and kindness. Her genuineness is a rare and precious quality that makes me want to snatch her up and keep her all to myself. So rare that my cynicism easily convinced me she was a master manipulator when I saw her at Sante's apartment.

I hate that I leaped to such a conclusion without any attempt at questioning the situation. I'm a fucking detective, for God's sake. I work hard not to make assumptions. Every day is spent focusing on facts and evidence. Her presence at his place was hardly concrete evidence of a master plot, yet I had no trouble latching onto the story with a death grip.

It's a lesson I won't soon forget.

Questions before assumptions.

Curiosity over judgment.

And where Sachi is concerned, always give her the benefit of the doubt. I'd be a fool to do otherwise.

"You carved that?" The older woman with salt-and-pepper hair gapes bright-eyed at Sachi from across the table.

Sachi nods, her cheeks tinged with an adorable pink flush. She's modest. I wouldn't say she's uncomfortable with people praising her talents, but she definitely doesn't seek the attention. Hopefully, she won't mind my need to brag on her.

"If you think that's impressive, you should see what she can do with clay. Absolutely incredible."

Sachi raises a surprised brow at me.

I return the gesture, confirming that yes, I've done my research.

Her answering smile says, *I should have known.*

I drop my chin a fraction. *Indeed.*

Oblivious to our silent conversation, the woman across from us continues. "I wouldn't even know where to begin. You know, I went to see the statue of *David,* and the museum has an amazing display showing the stages Michelangelo would have used to carve it. It's wild when you see it like that. This giant block of marble, and he somehow chips away until there's this perfect man—as if David had been there hiding in the stone all along. Absolutely incredible."

"Well, I'm no Michelangelo," Sachi hurries to say.

The woman's husband nudges his finished dinner plate forward and lifts his wineglass. "You don't have to be Michelangelo to have an amazing talent. Consider yourself lucky. Some of us have the creative wherewithal of a fruit fly. If I didn't have Leslie here to pick my clothes, I'd probably have to tell people I was color blind."

His wife waves him off with a delighted chuckle, then turns back to Sachi. "I'd love to hear more about how you learned to sculpt. Is it something you were just born doing, or did you develop a love of it later?"

"Actually, it sort of started with food. My parents came to the US from Japan, where my mother learned Tibetan flower butter art. For her, it was a fun hobby, but I really took to it. I started carving all kinds of stuff in butter. Fortunately, my parents were super supportive and encouraged me to pursue my passions. They sent me to all kinds of art classes, but sculpting has always been my favorite medium."

"Oh, how wonderful." She takes out her reading glasses from her beaded clutch purse and opens her phone. "You know I have to look up this butter art. I'm not familiar, and if I don't do it now, I'll forget." She taps at the screen with a single finger while her husband leans in for a look. "Oh, my word, that's gorgeous! I love the colors. I can't believe I've never heard of this before. I can't wait to tell the ladies at bridge next week."

A server begins collecting empty plates to prepare for the dessert portion of the meal. The table of eight breaks into several smaller conversations. I take the opportunity to lean over and check in with Sachi.

"You need anything?"

She gives me a funny look. "Like what?"

I shrug. "Anything at all. If you're cold, I'll give you my jacket. If you're thirsty, I'll bring you water."

Another delicate blush warms her cheeks. "And if I'm tired?"

"I'll make our excuses and escort you home, tuck you into bed, and give you a kiss good night."

"Just a kiss?" she whispers, peering up at me through her lashes.

My heart thuds in my chest. "Just a kiss."

"What if I want more?"

Fuck, this woman is going to make me hard in the middle of dinner.

"Then it'll be the one and only time I refuse you."

"Why's that?"

"Because I need you to want to see me again." And because I want her to know I'm interested in her and not just the sex. I told myself that this time around I wouldn't fuck this up, and that means showing I possess a modicum of restraint.

"Lure me back with the promise of sex?"

"Whatever it takes," I say without a hint of humor. "I don't want this to be the last time I see you."

Sachi bites her lip and nods. "We can talk about it later," she says quietly.

Her comment unsettles me, but I'm not going to push for an explanation. I'll have to respect her wishes and wait until the time is right.

Dessert looks way too fancy to eat. A slice of cheese-cake would have been better to me, but Sachi seems to enjoy it, and that's all that matters. As the final course wraps up, I go to the podium to thank everyone for coming and make the final call for bids on the silent auction. Any gathering in the name of the charity is always a fundraiser in one way or another.

Once the evening is over, I help Sachi collect her things and lead her to the building's entrance. Before we step outside to the valet, I slip my tux jacket over her shoulders, just as I did at the ball. I could have had a designer coat brought with the dresses, but I gave myself that one selfish act because if the night went well, I desperately wanted to see her in my jacket again. And now that it's happened, my chest puffs full of pride.

I drive Sachi home as promised and walk her up to her apartment. I even make sure there's no one waiting for her inside, since I know how easily that can happen.

"I had a really lovely evening, Dean. Thank you."

"It was the least I could do." I palm her cheek and graze my thumb across her smooth skin.

"Is this when I get my kiss?"

"Tell me I can see you again, Sachi." The words are a coarse plea. I wonder if I've been too gruff when she grazes her teeth over her bottom lip and lowers her gaze.

"I can't give up my friends, Dean. I really like you, and I want to see you again, but I can't if it means losing them."

"I'd never ask you to do that."

Her gaze snaps back to mine. "Really?"

"Absolutely. Loyalty, even among thieves, is still honorable. I respect that they're important to you. And besides, I'd never admit it to them, but those guys are far from the worst criminals I've come across."

"But what about your job? What if word gets out that you're associated with the Morettis? Even if only loosely?"

"People are gonna think what they want to think. You don't worry about me. I'll be fine, I promise."

"And what about my friends? You can't use me to get evidence on them. I'll never forgive you." The stern look she gives me makes the corners of my lips twitch with the need to bellow a laugh.

I hold up my right hand in oath. "So long as they don't pull out a gun and kill someone right in front of me, I swear I'm not going after them. There are plenty of worse criminals in the city to hunt down."

Again, she chews at her lip as though mulling over what I've said.

"Is it my turn?" I ask in a low rumble.

"Your turn for what?"

"To ask if this is when I get my kiss."

Her answering grin is magnificent. "Yes, please."

"Sachi Asano, can I have a kiss?"

"Yes," she breathes.

Fuck.

Yes.

I cup my hand around the back of her neck and hug

her close with my other arm, then bring my lips to hers in a sensual promise. An unhurried apology sealed with a pledge to be the best man I can be for her.

There are no guarantees in life. Only time will tell if this will work out, but I want to try because this incredible woman is carving out a place in my heart with every minute we spend together. And this thing between us has only just begun.

I STAND FOR SEVERAL LONG MINUTES WITH MY BACK against the door, grinning like a loon. I'm alone. Dean left after gifting me with the most sensual, reverent kiss I've ever experienced. It was so spectacular that I'm still lost in the moment. Still lost in the night that wasn't supposed to be. I was supposed to go to work, then spend my evening licking my wounds with mint chip ice cream and sitcom reruns.

Instead, I feel like my life's been turned upside down in the best way possible.

What Dean did tonight was a grand gesture worthy of

a Hollywood movie. I didn't think that sort of thing happened in real life. But it does, and I'm living proof.

More grinning.

Lights.

It's time to turn the lights back on.

I switch on every festive bulb in my apartment, then turn off the overhead light so that the twinkling colors are just as vibrant as the joy in my heart.

Once I'm comfy on the sofa, I call Dani because I can't go to bed without telling her everything. Aside from my need to share this excitement bubbling inside me, she'd skewer me with one of her paint brushes if I didn't call. She answers quickly because it's later than I normally call. After assuring her there are no problems, I walk her through the broad strokes of the night's events.

I'll just say this.

Every girl should have a best friend who squeals with delight on her behalf.

Dani is so giddy, her husband runs from the other room with his gun in hand, which I only know because she has to pause and assure him there isn't a home invasion taking place.

"Speaking of men with guns," I transition back to our conversation. "I want you to know I told Dean that you guys are nonnegotiable. I'm not giving up my friends for him, and he promised it wouldn't be a problem."

"I'm glad he thinks so, but nothing is ever guaranteed, and that's okay. No need to borrow trouble. We can cross that bridge should we come to it. I'm just glad you're willing to take a chance and see what happens."

"True, but I don't like taking chances when your lives are at risk."

"It's Tommy's choice to do what he does. You're not the one taking chances. He is. That's on him. But I get what you're saying, and I appreciate it. Just know that should something happen, you aren't responsible for the consequences of his actions."

Emotion thickens in my throat, making it hard to swallow. "Dang, Dani. When did you get so smart?" I tease to keep from bursting into tears.

"I've always been this smart. You're just now catching up." Her smug reply has me laughing out loud, as she intended.

"I appreciate your patience in the meantime."

"Not a problem. You know I'm fond of charity."

"You know what? I'm letting you off the hook for that one, but only because it reminded me that I haven't told you everything yet."

"There's *more?*"

"Oh, yeah. You know how I said Dean was at a charity dinner?"

"Yeah?"

"He's one of the founders of the charity."

"I'm not following."

"He's rich, Dani. Like, I think he might be super rich," I whisper into the phone. I'm not even sure why. I guess I don't want the universe to hear me and think I'm in it for the money. I'm not, but holy crap, it's a huge perk.

"He's a detective," Dani points out, still confused.

"Yes, but his parents left him a big estate. They were killed when he was young. He went into law enforcement because of them, but he doesn't need the money. The man is a real-life Bruce Wayne when he's not fighting crime."

"Ohhh..."

"Yeahhh..." I agree.

Dani's quiet for a breath before she continues in a choked voice. "I'm so happy for you, Sach."

"Well, it's early still, but I'm pretty freaking excited, myself." I grin. "You should see the gown I'm wearing. It's designer—all of them were. He made certain I felt like a princess tonight."

"As he should," she says in a voice strained with emotion. "You deserve to be cherished."

Her tears are infectious, causing my eyes to burn. "Thanks, honey. Okay, I'm going to let you go before I end up sobbing."

"I'm so glad you called. I have a really good feeling about this, Sach. It's going to be good."

"I won't argue with that."

"Hey, want to hang out tomorrow?" she interjects excitedly.

"I'm working at the gallery all afternoon, but I can stop by on my way in."

"Perfect! See you then."

"Bye!" I hang up and hold my phone to my chest, not sure how I'm ever going to calm down enough to sleep.

Regardless, I get ready for bed and curl up under the covers with *The Grinch Who Stole Christmas* playing on the TV. Not either of the newer ones. The old version. It's my favorite.

By the time the Whos gather around their town square and are joyfully singing hand in hand, I drift into my own Whoville dreamland.

THE NEXT DAY, I open my front door in a rush for work and nearly collide with someone in the hallway.

"Sorry!" I cry, pulling up short.

"No problem. I have a delivery and was just about to knock. You Sachi?" The deliveryman holds a large bouquet so picturesque that it almost looks fake. Red roses and holly berries pop with color amid a thick assortment of seasonal greenery—sprigs of pine, boxwood, and eucalyptus. It's a Christmas arrangement fit for a queen.

"Yeah, that's me," I say in awe.

The guy grins and hands over the glass vase. "Enjoy and have a happy holiday."

"Thank you!" I take the flowers inside, and my stomach hosts an entire colony of butterflies. Tucked amid the greenery is a note that reads simply, "You promised," followed by a phone number.

Before Dean left last night, he made me promise I'd see him again. I hadn't even realized I didn't have his number.

You do now.

I grin and tuck the card into my back pocket. If I don't hurry, I won't have time to see Dani before work. I decide to text him once I'm at the gallery, which ends up being a supremely dumb choice. I can hardly concentrate on a word Dani says while that card burns a hole in my favorite pair of jeans. After what feels like a lifetime, I get settled at work and pull out my phone.

Me: The flowers are gorgeous, thank you 🤍

He answers immediately.

Dean: Glad you like them

Dean: You have Christmas plans?

Me: Nope. My parents weren't able to make it this year.

As soon as I hit send, I worry if I shouldn't have said the part about my parents. Dean's an orphan, and I imagine this time of year is extra hard.

Dean: Me either 😶

Oh my God. He's joking about his dead parents.

Why do I think that's so sweet? He's trying to make me comfortable and let me know I don't have to tiptoe around the subject.

Dean: I always volunteer to work Christmas Day so other guys can be with their families.

So. Freaking. Sweet.

Dean: But I'm free Christmas Eve

It's a good thing there are no clients at the gallery because I'm staring at my phone with a grin the size of Rhode Island.

Me: My place isn't big, but you'd be welcome to come by and hang out.

Is it too soon for Christmas together?

Our situation is too abnormal for me to know what's reasonable. If neither of us has plans, why should it be different from having a date on any other day?

Dean: Your place is perfect—it's way more festive

I should have known he'd be on the same page. He's not the type to play dating games.

Dean: That's still four days away

Dean: Can I see you before then?

More idiotic grinning.

No games here, just an honest desire to see me.

Me: When are you working?

Dean: Tell me when I can see you, and I'll make it work.

Can a girl die from smiling too much?

I sure hope not.

Me: What about lunch tomorrow?

Dean: Perfect

NOT ONLY DID Dean and I have lunch the next day but we did so for the three days that followed as well. We even did a lap around Rockefeller Center and watched families ice skating under the giant Christmas tree. I wasn't dressed for skating, but he said he'd skate with me another day if I wanted to go.

I'm so taking him up on that.

But not today because it's Christmas Eve, and the city is expecting two feet of snow. But even more importantly, it's the first time we've been alone together since the charity dinner. I had to restrain myself when I opened the door to find him wearing a Santa hat. It was a smidgen crooked. And did I mention he has dimples?

I'm surprised I didn't strip him naked right then and there.

Christmas miracles do exist.

"Hey!"

"Hello, gorgeous. I hope you don't mind that I brought an overnight bag. I didn't want to look presumptuous—it's this weather. It's getting pretty bad out there, and I'm not sure I'll be able to make it home before working tomorrow."

"Not a problem at all. I'd rather you stay than go back out in that unnecessarily."

Please, *please*, stay.

"I appreciate it." He sets an overstuffed backpack by the door.

"Make yourself at home." I motion to the sofa, then

skip to the kitchen, which is technically just a corner of the living room. "I have homemade snack mix, homemade fudge, and ... wait for it ... homemade Babka bread. It's delicious."

"You made all this? I thought you said you carve food, not cook it." He stands behind me to admire the spread over my shoulder as I make a plate for us to take to the sofa.

"Never said they were made in my home. All gifts." I tear off a corner of Babka. "Try this. Dani's Gran makes it. I think she must be a witch because this stuff's magical."

When his lips take my offering and make contact with my fingers, my girl bits swoon.

His eyes dilate as if he knows. I clear my throat.

"Ready to watch the movie?"

"Definitely." He takes the plate and sets it on my small coffee table. Once he's seated, I sit next to him then gasp when he hefts me closer until I'm tucked up against him. "That's better."

"Yeah," I say in a dreamy tone. "Want me to turn the tree lights off?"

"No way. The lights are the best part of Christmas."

"That's what I say, too! Most people who see my place this time of year think it's too much, but I love it." Pride beams in my eyes as I take in the sparkling array of reds, greens, and golds.

"They're just envious."

"Right? You know, I was surprised you had a tree.

Seems like most single guys don't bother. I was a twinge worried you were married."

Dean chuckles. "Not married, as you now know. I always make sure to decorate for the holidays because it was my mom's favorite season. When I see that tree, I feel closer to them."

Did my ovaries just quiver?

"That's super sweet," I tell him quietly.

He pulls me a tiny bit closer and drops a kiss on the top of my head. "Talk about sweet. You better get that movie started before I get other ideas."

His gravelly words rake across my skin like a physical touch. We've kept our time together very ... *friendly* since the charity dinner, and the tension building between us is stifling. I appreciate his effort to be a gentleman. He's done an amazing job proving he's interested in more than my body, but my body's feeling a little neglected at this point. I'm ready to remedy that.

"Actually, I have a gift for you." I rise to my knees and straddle his lap, then lift my shirt over my head to reveal a sheer white bra trimmed with red satin ribbon, looking just like a present.

His strong hands squeeze my thighs. "Was tryin' not to rush things," he says through gritted teeth, his eyes glued to my breasts.

I slowly wiggle my chest back and forth. "Think that ship already sailed, baby."

"Thank *Christ*." Dean grinds his quickly swelling shaft

against my center, then gently takes one end of the ribbon between his teeth and achingly slowly pulls it a little loose. He doesn't undo the bow, just tests to make sure it's not purely decoration. "Best damn gift I've gotten in years. In fact, I'd like to admire it fully. Stand up."

The husky drawl of his gravelly voice is music to my ears. I eagerly do as he commands. Dean doesn't move a muscle. He remains leisurely lounging on the sofa as he peruses the landscape of my body.

"Show me all of it."

I slowly slide my lounge pants over my hips and down to the floor, exposing matching panties with red ribbon that ties on either side.

A masculine rumble of approval vibrates from deep in his chest as though he's a hungry lion surveying a herd of plump wildebeests. When he's finally ready, he rises to his feet with predatory grace.

I love the way he towers over me. So strong and confident. So controlled.

He tosses the Santa hat on the sofa and lifts his shirt over his head.

"The hat stays," I tell him, smirking.

"You *are* a naughty girl, aren't you?" He closes the distance between us and plants a sensual, languorous kiss on my lips. "Don't. Move," he says when he pulls away.

I watch raptly as he crosses to the gift wrapping supplies I have stashed in a bag on my kitchen table. I should have cleaned more before he came over, but maybe it's best he knows what he's getting into because neat and tidy, I am not. I believe chaos is like glitter—a pain in the ass to clean up, but worth the mess to have a little sparkle in life.

When he returns, he's got a spool of white curling ribbon and a pair of scissors in his hands.

"Hands behind your back."

My entire body thrums with excitement as he ties my hands together. Yet again, he walks away. This time, he goes to my Christmas tree and takes a candy cane from its branches. He then returns to trail the plastic-coated rainbow candy over my skin. He starts at my shoulder, down my arm and across to my belly before teasing along the edge of my panties. Then lower.

My heart skips a beat.

"Does my girl want a sweet treat?" He slides the hooked portion of the cane over my slit with only the sheer fabric of my panties between.

Diamonds have nothing on my nipples as they pebble impossibly hard with the need to be touched.

As if he knows, Dean takes the hooked end of the candy cane and flicks it over each taut peak. I gasp and press my chest forward, desperate for more. Every touch coaxes a storm inside me, but not enough to take my body where it wants to go. And he knows it. He's enjoying my delicious torture, so I decide to give a little in return.

I drop to my knees and look up at him imploringly. "Please, Santa. Can I suck your cock?"

Dean groans, and his abs flex. "That mouth, Sachi. How is it so sweet yet so filthy?" He frees himself, taking his engorged shaft in his fist and squeezing. "Show me what that beautiful mouth can do."

His free hand cradles the back of my head as he feeds himself to me, careful not to choke me.

He tastes so dang good, I'm ravenous. I lick and suck my man-dy cane like he's made of pure sugar. And when I hum with satisfaction, he lets loose a guttural moan, then pulls free of me.

"Enough," he barks savagely. "I want to taste you coming on my tongue."

He rips the ties from my wrists, then tugs the ribbons on my panties until the thin fabric falls to the floor. Once he has me on my back on the sofa, he hovers over me, untying the final bow between my breasts with his teeth.

"*God*, Dean. That feels so good."

He sucks my breast into his mouth, rolling his tongue round and round my nipple. My thighs squeeze with the need to fill myself—with the need for some sort of friction—but his giant body is in the way. Thankfully, he shows mercy and lowers himself to my core, where he begins to feast.

The man is seriously gifted. He has me hurtling toward an orgasm in no time. With my hand clenched in his hair, I scream my release. Wave upon wave of ultraviolet bliss radiates through my body while Dean milks me of every last ounce of pleasure.

Once I return to earth, he kisses a path up my body as I recover. I'm only partially aware when he raises my legs to fold me in half. I am fully on display for him. He drinks in the sight with my ankles in his hands, then trails the head of his warm cock over my sensitive flesh.

I hiss and writhe, though I can't move much in this position. When he finally sinks inside me, I feel like I've come home. Like everything is right with the world and life is perfect.

I wonder if he feels it too because he begins to fuck me with abandon, as though if he burrows inside me deep enough, he might be able to stay there forever. When he puts my ankles in a single hand, he uses the other hand to slide two fingers on either side of my clit. The sensation is divine.

"Dean ... I'm ... going ... to come," I chatter through his ruthless thrusts.

"Cream all over me, kitten. Drown me in your cum." He forces each word through gritted teeth, intensifying his movements until we both cry out in release.

Dizziness has me floating on choppy waters. Warm, radiant, bubbly water. I swear I see an entire galaxy of colors behind my closed eyelids.

Dean has well and truly rocked my world.

He eases my legs down, then rests his weight beside

mine, his large frame angled over me. "Guess we need a shower now before the movie."

"Mmm..." I'm incapable of speech.

I feel, rather than see, him smiling above me.

"I'll get the water running. You wait here," he gently teases. When he returns, I'm still in la-la land. He lifts me bridal style, finally drawing me back to life.

"Oh!" I wrap my arms around his shoulders and notice the snow raging outside the window as he crosses to my bathroom. "There's nothing better than a white Christmas," I muse wistfully.

"If it gets bad enough, I don't think I'll have to go in to work."

"Really?"

"Yeah, command will drop numbers to a skeleton crew. But if it's that bad, the city may be shut down for days." He sets me down in the bathroom. I keep my hands wrapped around the back of his neck, my sated body flush with his.

"Well, in that case, let it snow, let it snow, let it snow."

"I couldn't have said it better myself."

RECORD SNOWFALL SHUT DOWN THE CITY FOR THREE full days. New York hadn't seen a storm like that in fifty years. While that meant I got to spend Christmas Day with Dean, it also meant I didn't get to see my friends, so we decided to all get together on New Year's Day. Today.

It'll be the first time Dean has been around the guys since the showdown at Amelie's place.

On top of that, Dani's Mom and Gran are coming, too. It's brunch with the full crew, and I have no idea how it'll all unfold. I told Dean he didn't have to come. He worked New Year's Eve, so I know he's going to be exhausted, but he insisted. To use his words, what good does it do to make the city safer if it means abandoning the people who mean the most to me?

Sending me to brunch on my own isn't exactly abandonment, but I appreciate his desire to be with me at a time that's important to me. Even if it's for something as seemingly simple as brunch.

My heart works double-time as I walk in the chilly morning air toward the restaurant where we're all meeting. Mounds of white snow can still be seen in places, but mostly, it's turned into a sludgy brown mess. It was pretty while it lasted.

I'm the first to arrive at the quaint little bistro Amelie suggested. Early isn't usually my thing, but I was too excited to wait at home. I have to wonder if Dean feels the same when he's next to arrive with a coffee in hand.

"Hey, baby. How're you feeling?" I lift onto my toes to meet him in a kiss, his adoring gaze burning off the rest of the morning chill.

"All good, though I'm not sure why I feel like I'm meeting your father for the first time."

I laugh. "Glad I'm not the only one. It's strange since it's not like you don't already know these guys."

"Yeah, but I never cared what they thought before."

"You do now?"

"Of course. They mean a lot to you. That means they're important to me." He leans in and gives me another quick kiss while I melt into a gooey puddle on the floor.

"You get any sweeter, and I'm gonna get a toothache," I tease.

"No more man-dy cane for you, then," he teases back with a smug grin.

My jaw hits the floor. "How did you know?" I'm certain I never told him about our little term of endearment for him.

"Overheard you on the phone." He brings his lips close to my ear and murmurs, "Don't worry. I would never deny you your sweet tooth. This candy shop is always open for you." He accentuates his point with a snap of his teeth, sending me into a fit of giggles.

At the same time, Tommy and Dani, along with her mom and gran, walk through the doors. I give them all big hugs and introduce them to Dean. During the process, Sante and Amelie join the party. Dean shakes hands with Sante. Tommy gives him a lift of the chin. So far, so good.

Once we're shown to our table, Dean and I sit across from Sante and Amelie while Tommy and Dani sit across from her family. We don't even have time to pick up our menus when a loud bang ricochets through the restaurant. Us girls flinch while all the guys look ready for war. The instinctive reflexes relax when we realize the noise was a car backfiring, though Gran must not have gotten the memo.

"It wasn't me," Gran quickly announces. "I made sure not to bring my gun this time."

Dean mutters beside me, "I did not just hear that."

Dani shushes her grandmother. "Dean is a cop, Gran. You can't go saying stuff like that."

"It was a joke, right?" Dean asks, eyes cutting from Amelie to Sante. "She doesn't really carry."

"She's not afraid to use it, either," Sante confirms with a chuckle.

Tommy just shakes his head in exasperation.

Dean leans back in his chair with a sigh. "I knew I might hear shit if I was around you guys more. Didn't expect it to be about grannies gone wild."

The guys both laugh, cutting away any residual tension from the room.

"You must see all kinds of crazy shit working on the force," Sante notes.

"Let's just say I won't have any trouble coming up with topics if I ever decide to write a memoir."

"Come on, you gotta give us more than that," Sante pushes. "What's something off-the-wall nuts you've had to deal with?"

Dean narrows his eyes as though thinking back. "Last night, some drunk asshole froze his dick to a metal streetlight."

The entire table erupts in groans and laughter.

Dean chuckles. "Yup. He tried to take a leak and got tired. Thought he'd rest for a minute with his head on his arm against the pole, too drunk to realize he'd let his dick touch the pole, too. I had to pour water from a Solo cup on the damn thing to get it unstuck."

More groans.

"You still gotta do that shit even now that you're a detective?" Tommy asks.

"Everyone works New Year's Eve. *Everyone.*"

The guys grimace, then launch into a story about some guy they know who caught his own hair on fire with New Year's fireworks. From there, the conversation flows with ease throughout the rest of brunch. As soon as the plates are cleared, Dean sets his napkin on the table and scoots his chair out.

"I hope you all don't mind if we go ahead and cut out. I'm pretty damn tired."

"Hell, I'm tired for you," Sante says before standing and extending his hand for Dean to shake. The rest of the group shares the sentiment, initiating a round of goodbyes before we slip away.

"I can go back to my place and let you sleep," I offer once we're out on the sidewalk.

Dean drapes his arm around my shoulders, and we start walking. "No way. You're coming to my place. If I need to nap, I can do it with you there. Besides, I have something for you."

"Yeah?" If I smile any bigger, my cheeks will crack.

"Yup. Been waitin' all night to give it to you." He's not lying. His pace is lively despite his exhaustion. His excitement has me racking my brain over what the gift could be. I adore a good surprise.

When we get back to his place, there's a shoelace on the entry floor. It's strange because Dean is relatively tidy. He doesn't even leave his shoes in the entry, let alone a single lace. I pick it up just as a flash of white shoots across the living room floor.

"Dean? Was that a—"

"Kitten?" He takes the shoelace from my hand and dangles it over the floor, letting the plastic end clack against the wood. Within seconds, the fluffiest, most adorable ball of white fur comes bounding into the entry, going head over tail in a fumbled pounce.

"Oh my God," I breathe, dropping to sit cross-legged on the floor. "Is this for me?" While I have a mini emotional breakdown, the kitten climbs into my lap, then leaps back out.

Tears fill my eyes.

"You said you always wanted a pet," Dean answers softly, joining me on the floor.

I think back and realize I did mention it back at the charity dinner. He remembered.

"But we've only known each other a couple of weeks." I'm so stunned that I can't help but question how this is possible. How could I end up with a man who wants nothing more than to make me happy, regardless of rules and social norms?

"And?" he asks, as if proving my point. He takes the

tiny fluff ball in his giant hand and holds it out to me. "It's a girl. She's only eight weeks old, but she does well going in a litter box."

"Of course, she does." I take her and cuddle her to my chest. "My sweet princess is perfect. Aren't you, precious?" I smother her in kisses, and she starts to purr.

When I look back at Dean, tears are pooled in my eyes. "You tryin' to make me fall for you, Dean Malone? Because I think it's working."

He hooks his hand around the back of my neck and pulls my lips to his for a kiss.

"Good. I don't want to fall alone."

We kiss again until the kitten gets bored and squirms free. I pull back to watch her bound away.

"What are we going to call her?"

"Your cat, your choice."

"Hmm ... she's very white."

"Cool Whip?" His playful suggestion has me laughing out loud.

"Good one, but not sure it's quite right."

"You can't do Snowball or something common like that."

"Obviously. It could be something Christmassy, since that's the season," I muse, watching as the kitten bats at a red ball Dean must have gotten her. The sight gives me an idea. "What about Cindy Lou Who?" I asked excitedly. "She looks just like her with those big blue eyes when

Cindy Lou holds the big red ornament that fell off her tree."

"I think it's perfect." Dean flashes a crooked smile. "Welcome home, Lou Lou."

His nickname has me grinning ear to ear. "Will she be staying here or at my place?"

"Either. Both. Whatever you want."

I consider the options. "She'd have more room here, but I'll miss her if she's not with me."

"Hmm, it's a tricky situation. Might mean you have to move in here."

"Dean!" I gape at him. "Were you planning to suggest that all along?"

He shrugs, mischief glinting in his azure eyes. "I would never."

I shove his chest playfully. He grabs my wrists and pulls me on top of him as he rolls back to lie on the wood floors, laughter filling his chest.

"Happy New Year, baby." His adoring gaze sweeps reverently across my face. "Hope it's the best year ever."

I beam down at him, bringing my lips a breath away from his. "With you in my life, I don't know how it couldn't be." Then I kiss him with every ounce of love pouring from my soul.

This is a wonderful life.

Thank you so much for reading *Mistletoe Masquerade*! *The Moretti Men* is a series of interconnected standalone novels. If this was your first foray into my writing, and you're interested in more, I'd suggest the following options:

1. Devil's Thirst (*The Moretti Men*, book 1)
2. Silent Vows (*The Byrne Brothers*, book 1)
   *Read more about each option below.

Missed the first *Moretti Men* novel?
Devil's Thirst (*The Moretti Men* #1)
Amelie is a ballerina with a stalker problem ... and a gorgeous but terrifying new neighbor who insists he can keep her safe. Too bad for her, she has no idea the two are one in the same.

Silent Vows (The Byrne Brothers #1)

Conner chose his arranged marriage bride because she was mute, thinking he wouldn't ever have to talk to her. But when he learns Noemi was silent to protect herself from an abusive father, he becomes obsessed with his new wife and vengeance on her behalf.

Stay in touch!!!

Make sure to join my newsletter and Facebook group to keep in touch!

ABOUT THE AUTHOR

Jill Ramsower is a life-long Texan—born in Houston, raised in Austin, and currently residing in West Texas. She attended Baylor University and subsequently Baylor Law School to obtain her BA and JD degrees. She spent the next fourteen years practicing law and raising her three children until one fateful day, she strayed from the well-trod path she had been walking and sat down to write a book. An addict with a pen, she set to writing like a woman possessed and discovered that telling stories is her passion in life.

Release Day Alerts, Sneak Peak, and Newsletter

To be the first to know about upcoming releases, please join Jill's Newsletter. (No spam or frequent pointless emails.)

Official Website: www.jillramsower.com
Jill's Facebook Page: www.facebook.com/jillramsowerauthor
Reader Group: Jill's Ravenous Readers
Follow Jill on Instagram: @jillramsowerauthor
Follow Jill on TikTok: @JillRamsowerauthor